## "You think I would come here to parade myself in a line of men hoping to become your king?"

"No. You had your chance at that position once, I suppose. But you decided against it, didn't you?" She let a small hard laugh escape her lips. "It would have been nice to have been informed of your feelings before you disappeared without a trace, leaving me in a cloud of scandal, of course."

"Minerva."

She turned back to face him, fully intending to continue the speech she had practiced over and over in her mind for months after he'd run from his duty. After he'd run from *her*. Liro deserved to know exactly how awful it had been. But he stepped closer without her realizing so that instead of a safe distance between them, she somehow wound up pressed flush against his chest.

**Amanda Cinelli** was born into a large Irish Italian family and raised in the leafy-green suburbs of County Dublin, Ireland. After dabbling in a few different career paths, she finally found her calling as an author upon winning an online writing competition with her first finished novel. With three small daughters at home, she usually spends her days doing school runs, changing diapers and writing romance. She still considers herself unbelievably lucky to be able to call this her day job.

### Books by Amanda Cinelli

### Harlequin Presents

#### *Monteverre Marriages*

*One Night with the Forbidden Princess*
*Claiming His Replacement Queen*

#### *Secret Heirs of Billionaires*

*The Secret to Marrying Marchesi*

#### *The Avelar Family Scandals*

*The Vows He Must Keep*
*Returning to Claim His Heir*

#### *The Greeks' Race to the Altar*

*Stolen in Her Wedding Gown*
*The Billionaire's Last-Minute Marriage*
*Pregnant in the Italian's Palazzo*

Visit the Author Profile page
at Harlequin.com for more titles.

# *Amanda Cinelli*

---

## A RING TO CLAIM HER CROWN

HARLEQUIN

PRESENTS

Recycling programs
for this product may
not exist in your area.

ISBN-13: 978-1-335-59273-6

A Ring to Claim Her Crown

Copyright © 2023 by Amanda Cinelli

For questions and comments about the quality of this book,
please contact us at CustomerService@Harlequin.com.

Harlequin Enterprises ULC
22 Adelaide St. West, 41st Floor
Toronto, Ontario M5H 4E3, Canada
www.Harlequin.com

Printed in U.S.A.

# A RING TO CLAIM HER CROWN

For my grandmother Elda, who loves to read my books when they come out in Italian—even if they are a little spicy!

Ti voglio bene, Nonna

# PROLOGUE

AT THE RIPE old age of nineteen-and-a-half, Crown Princess Minerva of Arqaleta was quite sure that she was completely immune to any kind of romantic attraction. She certainly wouldn't do something so foolish as fall in love with the surly, redheaded prince she was destined to marry.

The old-fashioned betrothal agreement between her mother and the King of Cisneros had begun when she'd been fourteen and, every year since, Minerva had obeyed and undertaken her scheduled four-week summer visit with Prince Oliveiro. There could be no two people more opposite in this world forced to spend weeks together in one another's company. Minerva despised reading and she despised silence and, by the time that first summer had come to an end, she'd been pretty sure she despised Prince Oliveiro too.

But…when she and the Prince had set eyes upon one another at this year's summer garden party… everything had changed.

A simple dance had turned into hours of talking and soon she'd found herself introducing him to her favourite place in all of Arqaleta, a teardrop-shaped lake on the edge of the palace grounds. She had found it when seeking out an errant arrow as a small child and had taken it upon herself to cut back most of the thorns and weeds, cleaning and polishing the old stone benches and statues and stringing up solar-powered fairy lights.

She told him all of this in a flurry of nerves as he took in every inch of her den, not knowing why it was so vital that he liked it, but that it was. She needed him to love this place just as much as she did. As usual, he hadn't spoken much, but, as he'd taken in the lake and the full moon reflecting upon the calm waters, she'd noticed his body visibly relax.

'It's so peaceful,' he'd whispered. 'Like we're the only two people in the world.'

Then he'd turned to her, their eyes meeting in the glow of twinkling lights, and everything else had ceased to exist. No duty, no differences, no watchful parents…it had just been them, boy and girl… Her hands had trembled in his as she'd closed the space between them and pressed her lips against his. Her first kiss…and his too, he'd later confessed.

They'd kissed for so long, her lips had felt swollen and her body had ached. He'd stopped every so often, staring down at her as though he were afraid she'd disappear at any moment. Then he'd taken her lips again, their bodies writhing against one another in the dark.

He'd asked her to call him 'Liro' that night—a name that only his mother had used for him, before her passing when he'd been a young boy. A name his father forbade him to use, as he did with everything that reminded him of the beloved wife he had lost.

He could barely look at the son who resembled her so closely. No one else knew of the name. For the first time, she'd seen a glimpse of something wild and furious beneath Liro's silent exterior. He was like an animal confined to a cage, pacing the length of the bars, consumed with the possibility of breaking free.

Their secret lakeside meetings became a nightly ritual over the following weeks. In the dark, she soon found herself offering up her own secrets too. Such as the long-drawn-out truth behind her parents' supposedly amicable divorce and her father's subsequent abandonment of her in favour of his new family. Liro always listened, her hand cradled in his.

They had never once spoken of the marriage arrangement that bound them, but she always felt it hang between them like a gauntlet of sorts. She knew that this summer eventually had to end and, when it did, Liro would leave. Only, this time, he would leave for obligatory military training in his home kingdom for two whole years and she would go to university in America. They'd be half a world away from one another.

On their last night together, she went ahead of him to the lake and waited, her mind swimming with all of the fears she'd tried to ignore. Would he think of her? Would he visit? Or would he abandon her without a thought, just like her father had?

That last thought stopped her in her tracks. Her own parents' marriage had been a royal arrangement, a public front for the good of the kingdom and their allies. As a child she'd been unaware of the tension but, as she'd grown older, their turbulent relationship had become impossible to ignore or escape. She had witnessed Papa's misery and resentment grow with each year he'd spent playing his role of King Consort.

Once they'd completed the terms of their betrothal…would Liro grow to feel the same way about her?

Her increasingly anxious thoughts were interrupted when Liro appeared at the lake's edge and made his way towards her in the moonlight. There were no lamps—nothing but the glow of the moon to illuminate the stern set of his mouth as he came to a stop a few feet away. She moved towards him, reaching up to claim his lips in a kiss, only to find his movement stilted and off.

'What's wrong?' she demanded, tightening her grip on his hand in a firm squeeze. His fingers were cold and he didn't squeeze her back.

'My father is here.'

Minerva inhaled sharply at the news, instantly understanding the change in him. King Guillermo didn't usually join his son in Arqaleta. Liro despised his father and they had spoken of him often, now that Liro actually spoke to her. She reached out to touch his shoulder, only for him to turn away and pace towards the lake.

'My father came to the archery arena yesterday to seek me out and instead he saw us...'

Minerva fought the wild urge to clap a hand across her mouth and scream like one of the characters in her mother's favourite soap operas. Liro had accompanied her to practice to watch her as usual, but then her best friend Bea had cancelled and unexpectedly they'd had the whole arena to themselves... She had barely taken a breath before both of them had been semi-undressed and writhing against one another on a pile of soft mats behind one of the equipment lockers.

Only, instead of stopping at the usual point of safety, for the first time they had gone all the way— another first for them both. It had felt special. A uniquely real and private moment in a life where so much had to be prearranged and approved by others.

Now, to learn that they'd been seen, and by King Guillermo of all people... She felt her stomach turn. For all that Arqaleta had become more modern and free, the kingdom of Cisneros was old and staunchly traditional in its culture. Would she be blamed for corrupting their son?

'What did he say?' She squared her shoulders, all trace of the previous excitement fully quashed by the reality of their situation. She noticed how Liro avoided her eyes, how his hands were clenched together so tightly the knuckles glowed white.

'He said he would speak to the Queen…' Liro's eyes searched hers. 'That we would need to be married straight away in case there was a child.'

'We were completely safe.' Minerva shook her head, furious. 'How dare he act as though we are a pair of errant children in need of punishment?'

A strange emotion shifted across Liro's face. 'Is that really how you would view marriage to me, Min? As a punishment?'

'That came out wrong.' Minerva inhaled a deep breath. 'What I mean is that it's too soon. I thought we would have years before we fulfilled the royal betrothal agreement.'

Liro's handsome features hardened at her words, his voice a low whisper in the semi-darkness. 'You knew about the agreement?'

'Of course,' she said, unnerved. 'Wait…you didn't?'

He shook his head once and Minerva felt her insides twist. He was utterly miserable at the revelation, that much was very clear.

'How long…?' He paused, clearing his throat.

'How long have you known that you were going to be forced to marry me some day?'

Minerva shivered in the cool breeze. This reminder of their reality was cold and wrong, his words slicking over her skin like ice water. 'I overheard them discuss the details on the day that you arrived, that very first summer.'

'Well…tonight is the first I heard of it.' He remained silent and still, his eyes scanning her with disbelief.

'I thought that you knew. I thought that was why you were so remome at first. You argued with your father that first day…you seemed so unhappy.'

'I *was* unhappy. I'm the youngest of three sons with a miserable father who only bothers to interact with his heir and his spare. Not to mention I'm the spitting image of the woman he can't bear to think about.' He closed his eyes and shook his head, a pained expression crossing his fair features. 'My father is unhinged. He's demanding that we get married as soon as possible, Minerva.'

She froze in his arms, a strange humming beginning in her ears. She'd been raised to believe that they were a progressive kingdom, that she would be free to rule as she saw fit whenever her time came. That she was trusted to know her own mind, to make her own choices, to experience some of the world for a while without the weight of her duty.

'We're only nineteen,' she said, taking a step back

until she was fully out of his reach. She couldn't think if he was touching her, not when her body still hadn't caught up with the reality of their situation. 'I have plans to go to college, to compete with my archery. I don't want to give that freedom up yet.'

Silence fell between them, a fraught, empty sound filled with the suffocating weight of their situation.

'Who says we have to give up any freedom at all?' he said quietly. 'Why should we live by their plans and agreements? Why should we be treated as pawns?'

Minerva shook her head softly, 'Liro… I'm going to be queen one day.'

'You don't have to be.' He met her eyes, a strange wildness to his expression.

It scared her, that wildness. She took a step away, pulling out of his grasp and pacing towards the lake. 'Liro, I love my country, and I trust my mother's judgement. If this marriage is a necessary part of my duty, then I have to do it.'

He glowered down at her and for the first time she felt self-conscious under his gaze. She knew to others it might seem weak, always following the rules and expectations of her role. Of course, sometimes she got tired of being the dutiful daughter, the overachiever. She was only human. These last few weeks, during their stolen moments of illicit pleasure, she had been Min. She had felt free with Liro… Maybe once they were married they could have the best of both worlds?

'You don't *have* to do anything,' Liro said quietly. He took a step closer, taking her hands in his. 'Min...haven't you ever dreamed of running away to start over somewhere new? Don't you ever yearn for a life of your own?'

'This *is* my life.' She frowned, pulling her hands from his grip.

Liro froze, his expression becoming strangely blank. The light summer breeze rustling the trees was a cacophony of sound against the unbearable silence that had fallen between them. Minerva didn't know what to say in the face of his hurtful words. She'd known that he wasn't fond of royal life back home, but did he truly believe her adherence to duty meant she didn't live a life of her own?

'I've never dreamed of running away from this, Liro.' She waited until he met her gaze before continuing. 'I've had five years to accustom myself to the idea of an arranged marriage. I didn't plan for these last few weeks, but... I see it as further evidence that we will make a compatible couple.'

'Compatible.' He stared at her for a long moment, his eyes hard. 'These past few weeks... Was this some kind of twisted exercise to test out our marital compatibility?'

'Of course not.'

Liro made a cruel, scoffing sound, his anger

clearly the reigning emotion. For a moment she contemplated laying it all out for him—how she'd been fascinated by him every year and had yearned for his attention. How she'd never felt happier than she'd felt these past few weeks. But then that small voice from before returned, reminding her what happened when you allowed yourself to be vulnerable. If she wanted a sensible, arranged marriage that would last, she needed to keep her emotions at a safe distance.

'We can push for a long engagement.' She stood upright, forcing herself to look away from him as she tried to disguise the crushing disappointment from his reaction. Clearly, Liro was not okay with the prospect of marrying her. She took a deep breath and adopted her most practised calm, regal smile, ignoring the tremor quaking in her abdomen with every word she spoke. 'Who knows? It might not be so terrible. I believe it will be a good match.'

'Do you *want* to marry me, Minerva?' he asked, grey-green eyes pinning her in place.

'Of course I do. I've just said as much, haven't I?'

'Tell me why.'

She squirmed under his attention, hating every moment of this conversation. 'I l-like you, Liro. I think you would make a great consort. We've been friends long enough for our union to be…believable. We're both royals, we know what is expected of our roles. It makes sense.'

'You make it sound like a business arrangement.'

Liro scowled. 'Marriage should do more than make sense, Minerva. What else?'

His demand, coupled with the harsh quality of his voice, made her feel small and uncertain. Like that younger version of herself who had called her father's number every night to leave embarrassingly long voicemails detailing every moment of her day. She hadn't been prepared for Papa to answer one day and coldly demand that she stop. The realisation that her own father hadn't missed her the way she missed him, that he didn't wish to be a part of her life any more than a couple of obligatory visits a year, had been the most crushing rejection she'd ever known.

Somewhere, in the last few weeks, she had let her guard down and now Liro had got under her skin. She had begun to rely on him, to long for him in a way that was far too much of a risk for their polite, royally arranged marriage. She needed to make things right. Needed to pull this betrothal back into safer territory, even if it hurt.

'We seem pretty good together in bed, is that what you want me to say?' She forced a smile, hating the flippant words as they left her lips. 'What else is there?'

Liro stiffened as though she'd struck him. His eyes drifted closed and Minerva instantly wished she could take it back. She felt a rush of foolish words threaten to climb up from her chest, needy phrases full of hope and longing that had no place in a safe, royal arrangement like theirs.

His hands gripped her shoulders, holding her away for a brief moment as he stared down at her. He seemed tortured, undone with a riot of unspoken emotions.

'You deserve more, Min,' he said softly.

'It won't be so bad,' she murmured against his throat. 'Not if this is how it can be.'

Giving in to her own weakness, she leaned in to kiss him. No more than a few seconds passed before he groaned and kissed her back. He held her close, his grip intense and purposeful, as if he was afraid she'd disappear at any moment. He was usually careful with her, almost reverent. But this time as they tore off their clothes and began to make love it felt different, more urgent. She was still a little tender— it was only her second time, after all. But she didn't care, not if it meant they could stop arguing and just go back to *this* for a while. She loved how he made her feel. She loved being with him…so much.

Tears filled her eyes and she told herself to pause, to savour this moment before their relationship became public property, but his lips against her skin made her mind swim. Liro gripped her jaw, tilting her face up to claim her mouth in a hard kiss.

'I'll remember you like this, always,' he whispered. 'So wild and beautiful for me.'

Just for him. *Yes*.

She gloried in his words, in the way he held onto her so tightly. She *felt* wild as her body began to shake with the force of her orgasm. She felt it the moment he joined her, his entire body shattering in her arms. Afterwards, he held her close to his chest, not withdrawing or letting go until the chilled night air made her teeth chatter. They were silent as they walked back to the palace but she felt strangely light.

She'd never harboured fantasies of a grand wedding. But the idea of being Liro's bride…of having him as her husband…made her feel excited and vulnerable all at once.

He walked her as far as the palace gates, as was their habit to avoid being discovered, not that it was necessary any longer. His stiff hug and murmur about needing to take a walk to clear his head set off alarm bells in her mind but she shook it off, telling herself that she was just being sensitive. That tomorrow everything would be figured out. Liro's whispered goodbye against her lips felt cold and distant but she didn't question it.

She didn't question anything…until it was already too late.

# CHAPTER ONE

*Fourteen years later*

MINERVA FOUGHT NOT to fidget with the heavy diamond tiara that had been secured artfully atop her head. Pins dug into her sensitive scalp, a scalp that had already endured three hours of glamorous torture with the royal stylist. Her waist-length curls had been washed, trimmed and tamed into the world's most intricate chignon.

A mirror was brought in front of her to survey the final look and she made sure to show her gratitude. These people were premium artists in their fields; it wasn't their fault that their princess would much rather be in jeans with her hair up in a messy bun. Doing away with the various dress codes she had been raised to adhere to for every event would be her first order of business once she became queen. Well, perhaps after she'd made a start on her kingdom's myriad other pressing issues, but still, it was pretty high on her to-do list.

Before she had a moment to compose herself, a small army of liveried staff entered the antechamber, announcing the arrival of her mother. Everyone rose, even Minerva, as Her Majesty Queen Uberta of Arqaleta appeared in the doorway, looking effortlessly regal as always.

Her mother crooned softly as she took in the antique Arqaletan gold-and-emerald tiara and matching jewels that adorned Minerva's ears and neck. 'I haven't seen these pieces in such a long time.'

'Master Nasir decided to bring out some of the pieces from your original coronation events, in honour of your celebration.' Minerva bowed her head towards their elderly curator, the man who single-handedly had preserved so much of her family's proud history over the years, and took huge honour in holding such a position. Minerva felt the same sense of privilege about her own role in their country's history, messy buns or not.

Queen Uberta was celebrating thirty years upon the throne on the same day as her sixtieth birthday. While Arqaleta was usually quite busy in the summer time, with tourists and their world-famous archery festival, this year they were holding a week-long celebration to honour their queen's momentous double milestone. There were to be seven days of events, culminating in a grand ball.

She met her mother's eyes and saw an echo of her own nervous excitement. Aside from a select few members of parliament and their royal administration, no one in the kingdom knew what was actually in store for them this week.

No one knew that the Queen had decided to change history by stepping down voluntarily. And not for any dramatic or sorrowful reason, simply because she wished to retire and pass on the crown. All of their late-night conversations, all of their detailed brainstorming sessions, were finally ready to be unveiled. Once the announcement was made on Sunday night, everything would change. A new era for their tiny island kingdom would begin.

'You look beautiful.' Her mother's hand gently squeezed hers. 'Nervous?'

'A little,' she said honestly, seeing no point in lying. Her mother could read her like a book anyway. She'd always been shocked to hear so many other royals describe deeply unhappy relationships with the people who had raised them.

But, then again, her mama had been a queen like the world had never known, changing traditions and forging progress even after the scandal of a messy public divorce and her refusal to remarry for the sake of propriety. The thought of having to fill such perfect shoes was a challenge Minerva knew she would not fully reach, but she would enjoy trying.

'You will have to get used to these public speeches, my love; they will only become more frequent.' Her mother sighed. 'You've hit an Olympic archery target live on television. Surely that was more nerve-racking than a week of playing host?'

'That's different.' Minerva smiled sadly, not entirely sad that her archery career had come to an end, but still not quite able to talk openly about the world she'd left behind. She'd had a good run, more than ten years of relative freedom to pursue her passion. When the time had come to return fully to her duty, she'd made the transition with ease.

'If you are not nervous about the speeches, then it must be about our other plans for this week.' Her mother stood by her side, brushing a non-existent fleck off the bead-encrusted shoulder of her gown. 'I still think it's a little unnecessary.'

Minerva shook out her shoulders and walked to the full-length windows that overlooked the crescent-shaped bay of Albo, their bustling capital city. Usually watching the steady movement of the ships coming in and out of port was one of her favourite calming techniques but not today. The harbour was in chaos, with hundreds of wealthy guests who had chosen to travel by yacht, and the harbour master was having quite a time trying to dock them all.

One particularly gigantic black super-yacht had drawn a small crowd of onlookers as it came to a stop a few miles out from the docks, bobbing in the bay like a gleaming obsidian mountain. There would be more just like that one and whoever owned it, more wealthy politicians, celebrities, millionaires, billionaires and whomever else her mother had decided might possibly be an appropriate match for the future Queen of Arqaleta.

For, while this week was about celebrating her mother's reign, it was also about securing Minerva's image as she prepared to become queen. There had never been an unmarried monarch at the time of their ascent to the throne of Arqaleta and, with public opinion inexplicably at an all-time low for their crown princess, Minerva had no other option but to find a husband…fast.

'Mother, you know that a brand-new unmarried queen upon the throne would cause uproar. Especially when your early retirement is already breaking tradition. It is what must be done.'

'But what if we just—?'

'I'm not arguing. I've already done all of the research, spoken to countless advisors, and every one of them said the exact same thing.' She imitated the rasping monotone of Robart, their royal parliament liaison. '"A life of service and dedication to this country is not enough; the Crown Princess must show allegiance in the form of matrimony and the intent to carry on the royal line".'

Queen Uberta frowned. 'I had hoped that you would have found someone eventually by yourself… after what happened.'

Minerva turned away, unable to stand the hint of regret in her mother's voice and the memories that came with it. The sting of Liro's abandonment, and the fact he had not trusted her with the truth, still hurt deeply. 'I much prefer a royal arrangement. It's easier.'

For a moment she thought her mother might have something to say on that matter, but she simply nodded once and let silence fall between them.

Her mother had been shocked and horrified after discovering the events with the former royal family of Cisneros. She had apologised for entering into the betrothal, revealing that it had been Parliament's idea originally to strengthen ties with their neighbouring kingdom. An alliance that had quickly revealed itself to be a dangerous one, as the Cisnerosi crown was revealed to be heavily in debt, and King Guillermo a master in corruption and deceit. Furious, the Queen had insisted that their entire royal family, including Prince Oliveiro, be formally banished from her kingdom. Minerva had accepted her mother's apology, but she would be the first to admit that she had pushed the bounds of her own freedom further than she'd ever intended before all of that had occurred.

She had played competitive archery in every country in the world, spending more than a decade juggling her passion and her duty. An unforeseen result of which was that now she was met with resistance from Parliament, which was now questioning the suitability of their unconventional royal.

She was not oblivious to the news headlines that

had dominated the press during her many absences from the kingdom. She was portrayed as a flight risk, far more curious about travelling the world and having fun than doing her duty to her kingdom. Perhaps for the first couple of years that might have been true but, once she'd blown off a little steam, she had always strived to achieve a balance. She had made it her personal mission to show that she could nurture her own dreams and her duty as crown princess. That she could love both roles and be successful.

Her mother had wanted to give her an unconventional amount of freedom from the duties that would have traditionally been expected, such as waving from a parade carriage or shaking hands at gala dinners. But Minerva had never missed the more important events. Now, if she wanted to take her place as queen—which she very much did—she would have to choose a royal spouse to stand by her side.

But, as she gazed down at the thin rectangular speech-cards that the team had prepared for her, she felt another strange wave of unease pass along her spine—the same prickle of anticipation that had come over her earlier only now more intense. She shook it off, knowing that she should have slept later that morning and not gone down to the old archery arena to run circuits. She might no longer compete but there was no rule to say that she could not still practise.

'Are you ready?' her mother asked, extending her hand.

Minerva smiled, loving that this was one of the most famous images they had shown their people in the fifteen years since her father had left. They were a team—mother and daughter against the world. The Queen and Crown Princess of Arqaleta were an unstoppable force.

'Okay, let's go and find me a husband.' She laughed.

The garden party was in full swing when they arrived and Minerva was swept along a line of guests, greeting and bowing and accepting their well wishes. A brief moment of girlish excitement was allowed as she spied her best friend Bea, who had arrived to stay in Arqaleta for a number of weeks to work with the team at the palace's stables and horse sanctuary. They didn't get to see each other much nowadays, since Bea's work took her all over the world, and something within Minerva calmed a little at just having her friend home.

But, once they'd had a moment to reconnect, she was pulled away by duty once more. Her mother made a point of introducing her to a large number of handsome men, some of them recognisable celebrities or businessmen, some of them distant royals from neighbouring kingdoms.

She didn't consider herself classically beautiful,

whatever that meant, but she knew that her appearance was pleasant enough on the eye—proved as each eligible bachelor gazed upon her with obvious interest. Her anxiety simmered in the back of her mind as she made the required small talk with a dizzying number of handsome counts, Formula One drivers and heirs. But, as the time for her speech grew nearer, she felt her nerves peak and at the first opportunity she could manage she wandered off in search of silence and refreshment.

Someone appeared suddenly on her peripheral vision and she turned, readying herself for another bout of polite chit-chat.

'Good afternoon,' she said, finding a red-haired man with dark sunglasses standing a small distance away. 'Apologies if we haven't been formally introduced yet. You are most welcome to Arqaleta.'

She prided herself on remembering names but she was pretty sure she would have remembered this guy. He was quite striking…handsome, with a sleek trimmed beard, impossibly tall and heavy with muscles in a way that seemed to contrast violently with the fitted black tuxedo he sported. Perhaps it was his thick red hair, a rare colour in these parts. It was a colour that reminded her of heartbreak, even after fourteen years.

She shook off that ridiculous thought, far more interested in another subtle undercurrent of emotion coursing through her—excitement. She rarely felt any kind of attraction to others, certainly never upon first glance, but it was undeniable that her attention had been piqued by this burly stranger.

Minerva shook off the thoroughly inappropriate sense of physical awareness coursing through her and busied herself refilling her glass of ice-water. She certainly needed cooling down. She subtly assessed the crowd behind her, noticing her mother's attention was firmly rapt upon them. Could it be potentially that this guy was one of the suitors Mama had hand-picked? The thought wasn't entirely uncomfortable. Or at least it wasn't at first, until he spoke again, this time in a low voice meant just for the two of them.

*'Gracias, princesa.'* His voice was a low rumble, startling her out of her thoughts.

*That voice…*

Minerva felt a shiver run up her arms as some-thing within her reacted to his tone, like an odd sense of déjà vu. She frowned, taking him in fully. He seemed so very out of place in this calm, sedate gar-den party. As if he was merely adopting a formal fa-çade as a disguise of sorts, a temporary mask to fit in. She rather wished he wouldn't. She found herself wondering where those hints of tattoos led…if they covered his whole body…

Shocked at the direction of her thoughts, she took a step backwards, almost knocking over a large ice sculpture of two kissing swans in the process. The man reached out, effortlessly catching the sculpture with one hand and tipping it back into place.

Without a word, he reached out with his other hand to steady her. His touch was warm and soft, despite the fact that his long fingers appeared callused and scarred. He had the hands of a man used to manual labour, his forearms corded with the kind of muscle that came from heavy lifting. The barest hint of dark tattoos was visible along the cuff of one white sleeve, quickly hidden as he straightened and stepped back.

Minerva let out a sigh of relief and ignored the small protest within her at the loss of his warmth. All in all, this man was possibly the furthest from polished royalty that a person could get. Almost as though he had heard her thoughts and wished to affirm their correctness, he growled and subtly pulled open the top button at his collar.

'Apologies, I take personal issue with the necessity of strangling oneself in the name of high fashion.'

Minerva let out a sound that was half-laugh, half-squeak as a small triangle of curling hair was revealed inch by inch. That was it; she needed to move away before she made an utter fool of herself. Saved by duty… An aide appeared to guide her to get ready her for her speech.

'My apologies, I hope you enjoy the rest of the festivities.' She smiled politely, noticing that he still hadn't bothered to remove his sunglasses. He hadn't introduced himself either, but there was no time now as he lowered himself to a polite bow and she was guided quickly away. But, even as she put distance between them, the strange, unsettling feeling of anticipation remained. She fought not to look back, to get one more good look at him...no matter how intrigued she was.

Liro scowled as Crown Princess Minerva walked away from him. He had fought not to imagine how their first meeting might go. He had been prepared for myriad potential scenarios...but not one in which she politely smiled at him like a complete stranger. But, of course, no one else here had recognised him, why would she after fourteen years?

He owned a mirror—he knew that he hardly resembled his younger self at all. Still, he felt the need to down the remnants of his fruity cocktail, unsettled as he watched Minerva's diamond-topped chignon disappear into the crowd.

When the invitation had arrived, signed by Her Majesty Queen Uberta of Arqaleta, Liro had believed it to be a practical joke. Why on earth would the woman who had formally banished him want him to come to her celebration event? Of course, once his own righteous indignation had passed, he had realised that there was a far more obvious and infinitely more hilarious reason...

Her Majesty, like most of the rest of the world, had absolutely no idea of the true identity of shipping magnate Liro San Nicolau. His alter ego had amassed a fortune and mystery like none other, allowing him a comfortable anonymity that he had never known in all twenty years of his former life. He felt no sense of nostalgia because it had been Prince Oliveiro of Cisneros who'd spent countless summers here. But, while Liro was quite used to crowds gathering around the hulking, sleek black yacht upon which he lived exclusively, he was not used to exiting said vessel and becoming the centre of attention himself. The afternoon sun was not the only thing that had made him sweat as he'd adjusted the sleeves of his sleek black tuxedo.

He had waited for a breath before he had entered the palace grounds, every one of his senses piqued and ready to respond to the first sign of recognition amongst the crowd…but none had come. Murmurs of curiosity had been the predominant sentiment through the sea of faces, but none of them had shouted out his true name.

It had been fourteen years since he'd had last set foot on Arqaletan soil, fourteen years since he had come to this island kingdom for the last time before his lengthy exile, and it seemed that just enough time had passed to render him completely unrecognisable. Of course, he was not surprised, considering he had gone from a slender and pampered prince

to a labourer aboard an international cargo ship—
a job he still performed quite often, despite having
worked his way up to owning that vessel and numerous others, amassing countless headquarters around
the globe.

He had built his wealth from nothing, fuelled only
by pure anger and regret. Now, as he looked around
the manicured gardens of the royal palace of Arqaleta, he waited to feel an ounce of sadness or emotion at the events that had set his new course in life.

Memories of countless balls that he had attended
in these palace grounds came and went from his attention. He felt no sadness or regret about the time
he had spent here. He felt nothing any more. This
was not an emotional plot for revenge, this was simply business.

Having been banished from Arqaleta under his
royal name, he had been careful to avoid any trade
with the small country for the entire duration of his
rise amongst the shipping world, despite the kingdom's perfect placement in the Alboran Sea, midway
between Spain and northern Africa. Its unique position had long made it an enviable trading partner
and port and now, with recent plans announced, he
could no longer ignore it.

Over the past year he had heard murmurs of plans
for a large developmental tender in the works being
pitched by new up-and-comers in the parliament.

His own competitors had showed signs of readiness to jump at the first sign of availability.

So, when his secretary had informed him of an invitation to a week-long celebration of Her Majesty Queen Uberta, he had been able to see through the first flush of red anger that'd initially clouded his vision. After some careful research, he had discovered that Her Majesty had absolutely no idea that his alter ego had any connection to the young prince she'd once known. And as for her daughter the crown princess… He had no need to think of her at all.

He had chosen to come here to make connections, to hunt in the way he knew best. If there was a weakness in Arqaleta's parliament that he might exploit to his own advantage, he would find it. If there was an opportunity here for him to take, he would take it without question.

He stalked along the periphery of the crowd with ease, glad that he had decided against bringing any security. Guards and teams of assistants reminded him far too much of his father, and his business model was that he preferred to operate alone. Living on a ship, he had very little need for security escorts or personal assistants. He kept a skeleton crew on board to keep the vessel running, and he hired virtual assistants to deal with most of his correspondence. Most of his meetings were performed remotely, and any site visits were informal, quick things.

He was renowned for his unusual mode of operation: he did not throw fancy dinners or wine and dine potential clients or business partners. If he wanted something, he went in direct pursuit of it and he offered what it was worth. He did not play games and did not tolerate them.

He recognised numerous faces from past business dealings here among the elegant guests. That realisation should have filled him with pride at how far he'd come and yet, as the crowd pushed and the royal family procession moved out of his view, he felt more tense than ever.

Her Highness Crown Princess Minerva had been quite busy over the past decade, travelling the world as he had hoped she would. Her talent at archery had always astounded him every time he had watched her practice, which had been a lot, during the five summers he had spent here in his youth. He had enormous amounts of respect for her drive and the things she had achieved since...

The media had always had an unhealthy interest in the young princess, a fact that had not changed at all in present times, judging by the reporters camped out all along the boundaries of the royal palace compound.

He had watched from afar as Minerva grew from a beautiful, carefree young woman into a future queen. Still beautiful, but not the same girl whom he had followed around these palace grounds. With every interview that he had read from his tiny bunk, he had witnessed the irreverent sparkle in her eyes dim a little more. Even when she had won her first Olympic gold medal, the smile that she'd given the camera had never quite been real enough for him. It was a fact that had filled him with frustration and eventually led him to ban himself completely from keeping track.

He was self-aware enough to know that was what he had been doing. It had taken years to work away the remnants of his lovesick obsession. But work it away he had. He had taken on every extra shift available on board, working, lifting and hefting heavy ropes and crates until his hands had been raw and his body ached enough to fall asleep. His body had transformed and his mind had grown sharper and more able to manage the riot of thoughts and worries that always consumed him.

The work had helped. The solitude had helped. He was in control now, so the decision to return here to hunt down a deal had not been a difficult one. He was a businessman, after all. This wasn't personal.

He had the answer to his question when Princess Minerva once again came into view, her bright smile glistening in the sunlight as she waved and followed her mother out into the centre of the courtyard. He hadn't believed it possible for her to become more beautiful than she had been at nineteen. She had always turned heads with her tall, lithe build but, at some point in the last decade, she had stopped wearing her dark hair down in its loose, natural curls. She was always perfectly put together in tailored dresses and blazers, her brown skin glowing with just the barest hint of expertly applied make-up. It infuriated him. He had watched his own mother and brother undergo the same tightening down of their images, the same relentless attention.

'Every eligible bachelor in Europe must be here. We all know what that means,' someone nearby announced, speaking loud enough in a heavy Irish accent for Liro to overhear the conversation. He followed the voices, spying a trio of lavishly dressed men standing a few feet away.

'She's given up the archery now. I suppose it's time to start securing the line. Pop out some royal brats!' a tanned, blond man with an American accent answered, his smile much too wide for Liro's comfort.

'She'll need to find someone to marry first.' Another voice joined the conversation. The handsome black man leaned closer to the other two, his accent distinctly French and his demeanour one of supreme confidence. 'Why else do you think I accepted Queen Uberta's personal invitation?'

The other two men frowned, looking upon one another with shrewd interest. The Frenchman made a tutting sound as Minerva smiled brightly up at the stage. 'I wouldn't mind waking up to that face each morning, that's for sure. Game on, gentlemen.'

Liro felt a low growl in his throat and stopped himself from taking a step towards the men. Taking a deep breath, he tried to focus on the speech and ignore the urge within him to give the so-called eligible bachelors a piece of his mind. The sun had gone behind a cloud and Liro removed his sunglasses at the same time that the crowd in front of him moved forward.

The princess paused mid-sentence and her eyes became locked on him with a sudden intensity that made every fibre of his being stand to attention. She frowned, clearly trying to gather her words as the crowd waited with bated breath. He didn't move or turn away from her silent scrutiny. Instead he felt himself will her to look…to see the truth, as no one else seemed to.

For a man who had spent fourteen years cultivating his alter ego and burying his past, he felt no unease as he saw the confusion morph into shocked recognition on her delicate features. Almost in slow motion he watched as the ornate champagne flute she'd been clutching slid from her grip and fell to the floor, smashing into a thousand glittering pieces.

With recognition came a flash of fury in her eyes, so bright he thought she might send him into flames on the spot. Minerva had recognised him…and she was absolutely furious.

# CHAPTER TWO

OF ALL THE ways Minerva had imagined softly spoken Prince Oliveiro reappearing in her life over the past fourteen years, one where he had morphed into a fiercely confident hunk with arms like tree trunks had not been one of them. She didn't know what had caught her eye from the opposite side of the garden—perhaps a reflection or a movement—but one moment she was looking out at the crowd and the next she was pinned by a familiar pair of green-grey eyes.

Shocked emotion blossomed in her chest as her mind tried to make sense of what she was seeing.

Liro.

No. How could it be him? Her mind struggled to process the slow smile that spread across his lips. A smile that was unmistakeably Liro's, despite the changes in the rest of him. She went onto full autopilot, somehow managing to get through the rest of her speech without crumbling into a babbling mess on the floor. Her heartbeat still hadn't slowed down, but her hands began to shake a little less once she'd practically run from the stage and downed an entire glass of champagne.

He clearly knew that she'd recognised him, and yet he had not attempted to leave or approach her. Still, she felt his eyes upon her the entire time as she was forced to speak with various delegates and politicians. When the guests were called to the grand dining hall, she found that seats had been assigned well in advance by the event staff, her position flanked by some of the suitors her mother had selected. She took her seat near the top of the table, looked up and there he was, seated directly across from her.

Such was the width of the grand table that she could barely hear a snippet of his conversation with the elderly woman to his left, something about shipping lanes and the cost of transit. He smiled politely at the woman, but it was not his old prince's smile. This man was someone completely different. The young man she had fallen for had smiled with warmth and genuine affection, but this man seemed to exude nothing but cold indifference.

She hadn't realised she was staring until green-grey eyes met hers, and she saw the challenge in them, just as she had the moment she'd first recognised him from the stage. She had passed off her glass-smashing as simple nerves, but now she could feel her mother's attention upon her. *Stay calm,* she reminded herself. 'Crown princess' mode meant control and grace: *rein it in*. Was she imagining it or was he smirking at her ever so slightly?

As she listened to other guests comment upon his apparent success as a global shipping magnate of some sort, she felt her insides tighten. He was well known by his pseudonym, apparently, and had been leading a life of luxurious freedom upon a yacht. The same ridiculous, giant black super-yacht she'd stared down at from her bedroom window that morning. It felt as if fourteen years of repressed rage was building up through her skin with every bite of food she tried to force down.

How dared he? How dared he come here and use a false name, of all things? What was he up to? What was his motivation for blindsiding her this way? Revenge? She felt the mad urge to call the guards and have him thrown out of the kingdom all over again, just to see how it might feel.

Did her mother have any idea who she'd invited? Almost as soon as the idea entered her head she brushed it away: her mother had been the one to banish the prince, after all. Her mother had not played a role in his family's downfall, but she had heard rumours about those who believed Arqaleta had benefited from the fall of their neighbours. Perhaps Liro had decided to come for revenge.

Conversations blurred into one as dinner wound down and the guests began to move towards the lively band that had set up stage in the ballroom.

The clammy air was stifling as she moved through the crowd, smiling at the handful of faces she recognised. The band was a mixture of traditional Arqaletan folk music and a more modern sound, and soon dancers filled the floor. She politely refused one suitor's quick request to join in and waited a beat before slipping quietly through an archway to the main hall.

She had made it no more than a few steps along the lamplit corridor before a large, looming shadow stepped out from an alcove, blocking her path.

The scent of cool sea air and cedarwood filled her nostrils as she took in the utter absence of any sign of the boy she had once loved. It was not him, and yet it was. Really…how had she not seen it at very first glance?

His short red hair was bathed in the light from the candelabra above, burnished golden in places, but much darker than the strawberry-blond it had been when she had known him. Was that why she hadn't recognised him immediately? He had been wearing sunglasses too, a fact that offset the aquiline nose he had once so maligned.

Apart from that, his jaw was wider and covered with an expertly trimmed beard; he seemed broader everywhere, in fact, and more angular. The boy she had known had been tall but this man was huge. Large, taut muscles strained the shoulders of his jacket and the long cords of his neck. Prince Oliveiro could easily have been described as handsome, if a little awkward, but this man was brutally attractive. The fact that she had felt such an instant attraction to him without fully recognising his identity made her angry all over again.

'*How* are you *here*?' The words left her mouth in a furious rush, shocking her. She shook her head, holding up a hand to stop him from coming any closer. Or perhaps to stop herself…she didn't know. All she knew was that she'd woken up this morning, fully open to the idea of matrimony after fourteen years of bitterness and cynicism… And this was the day he decided to walk back into her life? Pain rioted within her chest, pushing against her carefully posed exterior. She was becoming unhinged.

'I received an invitation, princess. Just like everyone else.' His voice was still as deep as she remembered. But had it always sounded so menacing?

'So that's how you're going to play this…feigning innocence? Did you think that no one would recognise you?'

'No one did, not even you at first.'

'So what? You planned to come here as your alter ego? To accept an invitation as one of my suitors… after what you did?' Her voice broke on the last word, the final shred of her control now dangerously thin.

He stepped close, his eyes strangely devoid of any emotion, eerily so. 'I accepted an invitation addressed to my business name, nothing more.'

'You're lying.'

'You think I would come here to parade myself in a line of men hoping to become your king?'

'No. You had your chance at that position once, I suppose. But you decided against it, didn't you?' She let a small, hard laugh escape her lips. 'It would have been nice to have been informed of your feelings before you disappeared without a trace—leaving me in a cloud of scandal, of course.'

'Minerva.'

She turned back to face him, fully intending to continue the speech she had practised over and over in her mind for months after he'd run from his duty. After he'd run from *her*. He deserved to know exactly how awful it had been. But he had stepped closer without her realising so that, instead of having a safe distance between them, she somehow wound up pressed flush against his chest.

Instinctively, her hands rose to push him away… or at least, that had been her intention. And yet moments passed when she remained frozen in place with the heat of his skin scorching her hands through his dress shirt. His muscles felt hot and solid underneath her fingertips. He was so much larger and stronger than she remembered. What was she doing, feeling him up?

She looked up, saw the heat in his gaze and wondered if his memory was conjuring up the same illicit pictures that hers was. The same stolen moments of fervent, joyful discovery that she had tried and failed to forget.

'You can hit me, princess, if that's what you need.' He growled. 'Hell knows, I would deserve it.'

Was that what she needed? Would that make all of these ugly, tangled feelings go back to wherever she'd stored them all this time without him? That was what she'd wanted to do, moments ago. But now…she was staring up into eyes that she had never dreamed of seeing again. Soft lips that had once driven her out of her tightly wound royal shell and shown her what it meant to be just a girl—just Minerva. They hadn't needed anything else when it had been just the two of them, just each other.

She moved to pull away and felt his hands tighten upon her elbows for the briefest moment, holding her close. She held her breath, fighting to find just the right words that would cut him, hurt him, just as she had been hurt. But as their gazes met and held and that anger within her morphed into something infinitely more dangerous. Her breath seemed too much for her lungs as she waited, wanting everything and nothing all at once. A war waged within her as Liro's strong hands flexed upon the soft skin of her elbows, his nostrils flaring as he inched closer, only to pause at the last moment.

Something broke within her, splitting the final thread that had held in more than a decade of longing. It was so long since she'd allowed herself to let go. So long…and it was all his fault. She grabbed the lapel of his jacket, roughly pulling him down to her so that she could capture his full, traitorous lips with her own.

She kissed him with fury and a wild abandon that she had thought herself no longer capable of, filling the angry thrust of her tongue and lips against his with all the frustration she'd locked away. She was vaguely aware of his beard scraping her chin and hard, callused hands caressing her neck, trying to soften her…trying to calm the raging storm he had awoken.

But she had no patience for it. She growled against his mouth, pulling his hands down tight upon her waist, showing him what she needed and praying he followed suit. His answering groan was shockingly obscene and he finally gave in. He took control of the kiss, crushing her against him as one hand fisted in her hair to hold her in place.

*Yes*, the voice within her cried. *This*.

Liro's kiss was plundering, wild and infinitely more soul-shattering than any one of her illicit memories of their short-lived affair. He had always had the ability to get under her skin this way, awakening some fragile scared thing that he alone seemed able to coax out. He had always made her feel free. But, as his lips slowed down and her thoughts became louder, she did not feel free. Nor had she realised she was crying until she felt a tear trickle its

way down her cheek. Liro's gaze was unreadable as
he reached out to wipe away that single, mortifying
drop of moisture from her cheek.

'I didn't come back here to hurt you again, Min.'

*'Don't.'* She breathed, taking a step back, the spell
of whatever madness had just taken hold of her for
those few ridiculous minutes fully broken.

'Don't hurt you…or don't call you Min?' he asked.

'Both.' She gritted her teeth.

He straightened, a shrewd look entering his eyes
as he watched a couple exit the ballroom behind them
and wave in their direction. Minerva exhaled sharply,
realising how close she had come to ruining all of her
plans again. How close she still might be if she didn't
get rid of him before scandal had the chance to break.

'You need to leave.' She tried and failed to remove the slight wobble from her voice as she stood
tall and met his gaze head-on. 'You should never
have come back here.'

'Is this how you treat all of the eligible bachelors
your mother has seemingly rounded up for you in
there?' he asked with feigned nonchalance.

Minerva cursed inwardly. Of course he would
have noticed all the suitors who had been invited; it
would have taken a fool not to. That her mother had
likely invited him as a potential candidate for marriage was a painful irony she couldn't quite process.
Not when she had just kissed him in plain view of
anyone that might have wandered out.

'I think I'm entitled to feel however I like, considering you are the one who walked away from our betrothal without a single word.'

He inhaled sharply, looking away. 'I thought it would make things easier...'

'Easier for whom?'

'For everyone.' He met her eyes. 'But mostly for you.'

Hysterical laughter bubbled in her throat for a split second as she took in the sincerity in his features. Did he truly believe that? Did he truly believe that walking away from the girl who had given him her first kiss...her first everything...had been what was best for her? Of all the patronising, self-sacrificing nonsense...

This night felt like some kind of strange fever dream...or perhaps it was a nightmare. Nothing good would come of his reappearance in their kingdom, that was for sure. No matter what riot of feelings he had reawakened within her, she was going to become queen of this country. She had to protect them from scandal, and this man was a walking scandal directly tied to her.

'You need to leave,' she said again, harsher this time. 'You are banished from this kingdom; your very appearance here is in breach of the law.'

'I have business here other than festivities,' he said silkily. 'But, if you wish to have me publicly removed, my identity casting shadow over such an important week, that is entirely your prerogative, Your Highness.'

It was a direct challenge, there was no mistake in it. Her fists balled tightly at her sides but she restrained herself from delivering the strike he had asked for. She would not satisfy him by losing her temper. No... She would give him exactly what he had given her—nothing.

Pulling free from his gaze, she took one final look at his cold, stern expression, turned on her heel and walked away.

Liro watched Minerva run from him, knowing that he could not pursue her. Not after what he had just done. What on earth had he been thinking, following her out here? He should have given her some time and space... He should have walked away the moment she had recognised him. But something within him had refused not to at least speak to her. He had expected anger, maybe even disappointment. But, as far as long-lost-lover reunions went, that had been pretty explosive.

He stood alone in the silent corridor for far longer than was necessary, waiting for his body to relax, for his erection to subside. He had reacted to her like a horny teenager... But it really was not a surprise, considering their history. Being around Minerva had always been like standing next to a flame. He closed his eyes, calming himself and reminding himself that he was not here for her. He had spent far too long training his mind not to think of her, to dream of her. The urges to return here had taken months to pass, months of lying awake at night in the bowels of a crowded ship, his body tight with longing and regret.

He had been little more than a boy when he'd left this kingdom; maybe that was why he had not been able to resist confronting her with the man he had become. He'd wanted to see the look in her eyes when she realised he had made something of himself beyond the impoverished prince she had almost settled for. He had walked away from his title and built his own empire, leaving her here with her precious duty.

He had no idea what she would do, now that she had discovered his return. He'd have no control over her if she desired to punish him by publicising his true identity. He had come to rely far too much on his new anonymity anyway; he had always known the day would come when somebody joined the dots. But he had not expected his reputation to lie in the hands of the Crown Princess of Arqaleta.

It was quite poetic, really; he laughed to himself as he took long strides across the palace grounds in the direction of the old town where he had a meeting. It was comedic, really, that the woman who had broken his heart and given him the purpose to reinvent himself and finally walk away from his toxic father and their corrupt family might be the one to try to break him.

She wouldn't, of course—he had worked for too long and too hard to build his empire to the point where very little could take it away. If anything, the public discovering that he was actually a former prince would only elevate Magnabest's global status. Not that it mattered. He had already ordered his yacht to be readied to set sail. He would be long gone from Arqaleta before night fell. Once he had completed the true purpose of his visit, of course.

He shook off the riot of feelings coursing through him as he walked through the old cobbled streets that he had spent so many summers traversing with Minerva by his side. The capital city, Albo, was busy tonight. The tourist season was in full swing and there was the added excitement of the Queen's celebration and all of the wealthy guests. He would bet there wasn't a free bed in the whole of the kingdom.

He did not begrudge them their success, nor did he blame them for the downfall of Cisneros. But still, seeing the obvious health and happiness of the people here felt a little raw. Once the marriage alliance had fallen through, and Liro had walked away from royal life, his father had continued to destroy their kingdom's economy to the point of revolt. His two older brothers had been instrumental in navigating a path for Cisneros to return to Spain, dismantling their historic monarchy piece by piece, but Liro had made the conscious choice not to return to help.

He had invested in Cisnerosi companies and created jobs, but nothing more.

It had long been known that Queen Uberta was the main reason why Arqaleta did not make use of the shipping lanes that were so popular with most countries around the Mediterranean. Their enviable position in the Alboran Sea midway between Spain and Algeria made them an untapped resource that he was determined to get for himself.

If anyone was going to take advantage of this deal, it would be him. From the moment he had first heard whispers of plans to redevelop and rezone the land around the small harbour, he had been thinking of a way to try to claim it. So, when the invitation had arrived from Queen Uberta herself, he had laughed aloud at his own good fortune. Getting a meeting with one of the top politicians in charge of the rezoning project had been child's play after that.

The meeting was held in a private conference room at the top of Albo's iconic parliament building, a beautiful white marble-and-stone structure that had once housed army battalions in times long past. Arqaleta was rich in history like this: most of its streets were lined with the plaques of UNESCO historically preserved buildings and the people worked hard with government infrastructure to keep their culture preserved. Arqaletan people were proud and welcoming to the tourists who provided most of their annual income. They might not take well to the lengthy development and disruption that would come from his redevelopment plans, but they would come round to it once they realised the benefits. He was sure of it.

As the government officials talked through the details of the harbour project, he wondered how much they had even considered the balance between old and new, but that was not something for him to consider. He was here to invest, not preserve the kingdom which had done nothing but reject him and remind him that he was not worthy. He might no longer be the young, naive prince who had been sent here to carry out his father's bidding, but he'd still felt the sting of the reminder of his banishment with every step he had taken through the palace.

One politician in particular, an elderly man named Robart, seemed particularly eager to get him to name his price and cement his offer. As a lifelong silent observer, Liro considered himself to be a particularly good judge of character, and something about this guy instantly put him on guard.

'What does Queen Uberta think of this deal?' he asked.

As expected, the men and women around the table exchanged not so subtle glances, most of them directed towards Robart, who then took the lead in responding.

'Her Majesty has much to worry about, what with the unrest surrounding the Crown Princess's negative standing in public opinion at present. She is more concerned with ensuring that the royal line carries on. So we have taken the initiative in creating some new projects that ensure our kingdom is at the forefront of economic progress.'

'What is the nature of this negative public opinion?' Liro asked, using every ounce of his energy to keep his body relaxed and his expression slightly uninterested.

'There has been some unrest.' The old man smirked. 'She spent much time travelling as an Olympian—an admirable adventure, but not really one that instils confidence in the people.'

'A gold-medal-winning Olympian as queen makes them lack confidence?' Liro raised one brow.

'Her athletic prowess is impressive, but we are still a country of tradition. Her mother gave her life to this country from a young age. She married well and she carried on the royal line. Minerva's duty is to do the same, and yet she has not shown any interest in marriage or family. It's a bad look.'

'A bad look that the Queen is very occupied with trying to fix, it seems…' Liro mused, finally seeing the full picture. Minerva was being forced to marry to appease her people. The very thing that Liro had almost made her do a lifetime ago. He had walked away from her, from this kingdom, to ensure that she was not trapped into a loveless marriage of convenience.

'Congratulations to you, on being invited as a

potential suitor. You have your work cut out for you with the others. I believe the Frenchman, Jean-Claude, is a firm favourite with the public.'

Liro thought of the suave aristocrat he'd spied monopolising Minerva's attention over dinner and felt his fingers grip his wine glass to the point of risking shattering it into a million pieces. Was this truly why the Queen had issued Liro San Nicolau, a man she had never met, a personal invitation? Did she believe a mysterious shipping magnate to be a potential future king of her kingdom?

'I'm here to do business,' he snapped, pushing away a sudden vision of any of the other men he'd met this evening taking Minerva as their bride. The very idea of her being pressured to choose from her mother's selection brought a sour taste to his mouth, but he brushed it off, bringing the conversation back to the final points he needed to know about the deal before leaving without another word.

It was only once he had returned to the solitude of his yacht in the harbour that he allowed himself to sit and think upon what he had just discovered.

Señor Robart was clearly pushing the agenda of Minerva being unsuitable to mask his own dealings behind the scenes. He would bet good money that Robart was also the reason why the royal family had been kept out of earshot of this deal until it was far enough along that they could not refuse the cash injection that it would provide.

It was none of his business and yet, when his captain came to ask if they should leave, he found himself pausing the order. It was not his duty to care for Minerva or shield her from the consequences of her own life. He was not her fiancé any longer and, judging by the events of today, she would have a new fiancé by the end of the week.

If Queen Uberta had not discovered the truth behind shipping magnate Liro San Nicolau, what on earth had she neglected to find out about the others? Thoughts crowded his peace, agitating him as he stared out across the sea towards the palace.

# CHAPTER THREE

MINERVA TOOK A deep breath and stared bleakly at her reflection in the mirror. Even with twice the amount of make-up she would normally wear, the result of her sleepless night was still starkly visible. She had returned to her room the evening before in a haze of quiet shock, excusing her maid in favour of spending some time undoing the tiny buttons of her dress one by one. But, even after undressing and taking a long freezing-cold shower, she had still lain awake for the entire night staring at the canopy above her bed and trying not to think of the feeling of having Liro's lips consuming hers.

The thought of seeing anyone today while she was still so shaken up was unbearable. She'd half-toyed with the idea of faking an illness just so she could lie in bed. But that would only encourage her mother and Bea to come investigating, and she would already struggle not to tell them everything as it was. There was no need to tell them anything, not so long as their unwanted guest disappeared, as she'd told him to. Once he was gone again, she would relax. She was sure of it.

She'd hoped that her memories of their chemistry were exaggerated, that perhaps her nineteen-year-old self had simply been overwhelmed with her first experience of lust. But, of the small handful of other people she'd kissed in the past fourteen years, none had ever made her feel close to what Liro had. Closing her eyes, she tried to focus on the items in her wardrobe, but her mind kept going back to his words.

*I didn't come back here to hurt you again, Min.*

A harsh shock of laughter escaped her lips as she thought of just how ridiculous a statement that was. To think that he might actually believe that his sudden return to her life wouldn't hurt her just as badly as his disappearance had. Much as she had tried to put on a brave face as she'd headed off to college a free and single woman, she had lost a part of herself when Liro had left. It had reinforced some ugly thoughts about her own worth, having yet another man she trusted just up and leave her life without a second thought.

The Argimon-Talil women were unlucky in love, her mother often said. But Minerva refused to believe that what had existed between Liro and her had truly been love. Surely love was not something a person could just walk away from without a fight, without even a conversation? It was far more likely that she had simply been infatuated with him and with the excitement of their sexual exploration. He'd said it himself, that he'd thought leaving would make things easier. And it was even more likely that he had simply seen her as a summer fling, one he'd decided to run from like a coward once he'd discovered their betrothal.

She shook off her thoughts and slid her feet into her favourite ratty old sandals, the perfect accessory to the simple blue jeans and white T-shirt she opted for. Dressing casually at the palace while she was 'off duty' was a relatively new concept but, if she was expected to marry a complete stranger for appearances, she was pretty sure the people seeing their princess in a pair of jeans wasn't going to cause a scandal.

She wasn't against the 'gowns and tiaras' life; she was simply against the idea of needing to dress formally all the time. She didn't understand it, and she probably never would, considering she had been trained for this life from birth. But thankfully her mother had stopped forcing the issue and allowed her to get on with her own day-to-day styling, for the most part.

The palace was abuzz with movement, the remnants of the evening before being tidied away in favour of plans and preparations for the grand ball that would take place on Saturday night. There were no formal events planned until later today, when she would likely be required to do some social mingling and networking among the various house guests who had been invited personally by the Queen. She hummed to herself as she made her way towards the ground-floor dining room where they breakfasted each morning.

But, when she entered the sunny breakfast room, she found it completely empty. Frowning, she walked through towards the long patio at the rear of the building where she could hear voices. The morning sun was warm on her skin as she stepped out onto the stone terrace that overlooked the gardens at the rear of the palace. They never ate out here... She frowned, then noticed that a dining table had been set up and was filled with people.

'Darling, you're late.' Her mother frowned from her post at the head of the table.

'I wasn't aware that we had breakfast plans.' Minerva forced a smile, noticing Bea had even joined them, and was happily inhaling a plate of honeyed buns near the end of the table. Through a series of pointed looks, Bea alerted her to the tableful of eligible bachelors, and Minerva fought the urge to gulp.

'It was a last-minute decision,' Queen Uberta crooned. 'I thought a more informal setting would be nice for of our guests to sample some of our famous morning pastries.'

*Nice indeed.* Minerva took in the sight of the pretty blond Irishman, John, to whom she had been introduced the day before. By his side was the exceedingly handsome French actor Jean-Claude, and two spots down was Prince Lorenz, who quickly stood and pulled out a chair for Minerva to take directly beside him. She smiled obligingly and lowered herself into the seat slowly while still scanning the table.

Liro was not here. She had spent much of last night wondering what she might do if Liro did not leave as she had advised him to. Surely he had come to his senses and realised that his few moments here would only serve to endanger his new persona, and that she would not hesitate in revealing the truth of his origins? As she looked out to where the harbour was just visible in the distance, she felt a slight tightening in her chest, knowing that she would not see him again.

Breakfast passed with amicable conversation, with the trio of Mama's finest matchmaking selections still doing their very best to outdo one another with exciting tales of their achievements. Jean-Claude was quite funny and a born entertainer. John was charming, in a quiet kind of way, but the tall, dark and handsome Prince Lorenz seemed most intent upon captivating her.

He was well-educated and charming, without being overly confident, plus he had expressed a great interest in her charity work around the world with the Olympic foundation. He had been a former rower at university, and they shared a few moments talking about the psychological and physical endurance required for an athlete. He was the ideal candidate that she would've expected her mother to choose for her but, when she looked up towards where Her Majesty sat at the head of the table, she found her mother staring at her with a pensive frown.

'So sorry that I'm late—have I missed breakfast?' a familiar low voice asked from the stairs that led down to the gardens. Minerva turned to watch Liro stride towards them, looking fresh and unruffled as ever in a sage-green polo shirt and charcoal-grey slacks. Again, sunglasses shielded his gaze from hers and she did not even try to hide her annoyance as she narrowed her eyes upon him.

Was that a smirk gracing his lips as he passed her? He moved straight towards her mother, leaning down into a bow and accepting her hand to lay a reverent kiss upon it, as was Arqaletan custom.

'Señor San Nicolau, I was beginning to worry that you had abandoned your invitation.'

'I simply had a matter to attend to down in the harbour. It appears that a yacht the size of mine has garnered quite a lot of attention.'

'I was never one for the super-yachts myself,' the brooding Irishman, John, mused loudly. 'What is it that they say about those who require extra-large vessels?'

'Over-compensating?' someone mused, earning a low murmur of uneasy laughter.

'Considering he owns most of the largest vessels in the world, I would shudder to think what he's over-compensating for,' Bea suggested loudly from the end of the table. Minerva coughed on the mouthful of croissant she'd just bitten into, eyes watering.

Liro smiled good-naturedly, laughing along easily as he sat down and removed his sunglasses. When his eyes met hers for a split second, Minerva felt her traitorous stomach flip.

'There is no need for you to stay on your ship—we have ample room here.' Her mother spoke over the din. 'In fact, it is considered the height of bad manners to refuse my invitation.'

'I understand, Your Majesty, truly I do,' he said 'But my yacht is my headquarters. I live there fifty-two weeks of the year and it is the best place for me to find a balance between work and…pleasure.'

Minerva ignored the hum of awareness that vibrated through her at the emphasis he placed upon that final word.

'An honourable decision.' Her mother nodded. 'I find a strong work ethic to be *such* a valuable quality.'

Minerva looked for any sign of recognition in her mother's serene features but it appeared she had no idea that the man she was praising was the same young prince she had banned from ever returning to their kingdom. Looking at how much he had changed physically, she supposed not many would see the similarities. He bowed his head once again in deference and Minerva fought the urge to roll her eyes. She could feel Liro's gaze boring into her, so she made extra efforts to renew the conversation with Prince Lorenz, laughing politely at his admittedly bland joke and offering to give him a lesson in target practice whenever he needed.

Once breakfast had finished, Minerva made to excuse herself, only to find the stable master striding across the lawns to inform her that their horses had been readied for the morning's excursion.

'Let me guess,' Minerva said to her mother. 'You forgot to tell me about that as well?'

Queen Uberta shrugged one delicate shoulder and sipped her tea.

Bea ran ahead to perform her morning checks on one of the newly rescued stallions with which she was working, who had become ill during the night. Minerva stood up, looking down at her mother, and tried to convey with her eyes as much as possible her absolute intention to have a very stern conversation once this day came to an end. She sighed with resignation as their group was guided down towards the stables.

Minerva rode her own horse, an impressively fast and agile white stallion named Grumpy that she'd raised herself from a foal with Bea's expert guidance. Most of their party opted for quieter horses, but she was unsurprised to see the selections of the three men who she'd begun referring to internally as 'The Suitors'. It was an old-fashioned term and one that felt entirely apt for this week's objective. She'd already whittled the larger crowd of eligible bachelors down to three. By the end of this week, she would be choosing one of them for marriage.

She tried not to stare as Liro opted for a politely tempered grey-speckled mare by the name of Strawberry who he proceeded to croon to in a low voice as he watched the stable hand ready her. They had all taken a moment to dress in clothes appropriate for riding apart from her, so Minerva slipped away to change in the changing rooms.

When she exited, all eyes were on her, and she fought not to squirm under the scrutiny. It was rather impossible to mount a horse without sticking out one's behind.

But, as she watched Liro slide one booted foot into a stirrup and effortlessly haul himself into position, she herself fought not to stare. His thighs were like tree trunks in the dark jodhpurs he wore like a second skin. His sage-green polo shirt had now been covered with a perfectly tailored black riding jacket, a matching helmet sat proudly atop his head. The overall effect made him look even more gigantic and intimidating, despite him having chosen a modest mount. The three other men flanked him upon their giant black and brown stallions, and Minerva could not miss the measuring looks upon their faces as they gazed upon their competition. If only they knew that Liro was no competition at all.

*I did not come for you.*

Once again that tight ball in her chest throbbed but she ignored it, kicking a heel back to guide her horse forward and leading their small group along a path that wound around the palace. They reached a crossroads, and for a moment Minerva contemplated taking them on the leisurely wandering path that best showcased the striking views down to the coastline. But then she remembered the smug look upon Liro's face when she'd seen him at breakfast and she instantly guided her horse to the right, down towards the rockier forest path.

'Hope you can all keep up, gentlemen.' She smiled innocently, taking off at a canter.

Liro was fast regretting his decision to return to the palace this morning. He should have stuck to his original plan and set sail the night before—in fact he wasn't quite sure why he had stayed. And he certainly had no idea what had possessed him to attend the breakfast this morning and join this ridiculous outing of socialites.

The Frenchman was getting on his nerves. Minerva laughed again at the charming actor, giving him her full attention. What on earth could he be saying that was so funny anyway?

He adjusted himself in his seat, trying to relax the death grip of his thighs around the wide barrel of the sturdy mare's back. He had never been a strong rider as a boy, and of course there was no real use for horse-riding skills when one lived at sea. But it appeared his new strength meant he was slightly more competent than he had once been. Still, the jostling and moving beneath him made him immeasurably nervous, a sensation that he'd rarely experienced in the past decade.

The other riders evidently noticed his discomfort, the Irishman passing a joke about him not having his sea legs. If it had been the Frenchman, perhaps he would have shown him exactly how balanced he felt; the charmer wouldn't last a moment on one of his ships. But the other two seemed like nice guys—decent, at the very least.

Still, he had ordered a private in-depth investigation into the three men to deduce exactly what had brought them here. He could have left it there, and sent on any information to Minerva anonymously in the event that she did actually choose one of these men as her...king consort. The word left a sour taste in his mouth. There had been no reason for him to remain, and yet here he was.

From the moment Minerva had emerged from the dressing room in her skin-tight leggings and perfectly fitted black polo-shirt, Liro had been on edge. She had the perfect form for every sport, it appeared:

the way she'd mounted the horse with effortless grace had made his teeth grind together. And, even as he concentrated on questioning the other men under the guise of casual conversation, his eyes never strayed from her for long.

Minerva had the perfect balance of strength and curves, her long, lean frame sitting so proudly atop her mount. Her dark hair had been wound up into a tight bun beneath her riding hat, putting the full length of her neck on display. He remembered trailing a kiss down that neck the night before, right before she had pushed him away. The scent of her had lingered upon his dress shirt long after he had returned to the yacht, and he had only barely resisted burying his face into it to find some relief.

He was not a horny teenager any longer, he was a grown man, and he was here to ensure that nothing would affect his business deal, nothing more. He needed to know exactly what was going on here between the Crown Princess's supposed dilemma and the likely corrupt politicians in the capital. He needed to know if there was a connection between the two before he proceeded any further.

*And, if you find out that there is no connection, what then?* a small voice asked. What if he discovered that all was well here in this kingdom, and that the only thing threatening her happiness was his reappearance?

That thought bothered him more than it should

have, leaving him scowling into the distance so much that he almost missed the sharp redirection of the party in front of him, down a rocky outcrop from the beaten path.

'Princess, are you sure that this is the best path for our party?' her usually eternally carefree and optimistic friend Beatriz called out, concern in her voice. 'You know how tricky this trail can be.'

'If anyone is not a confident rider, they are free to stay above on the easier path,' Minerva said sweetly, throwing an unmistakable glance back towards Liro.

Ah. He had wondered when his punishment would begin. Liro fought not to smile as he raised one brow in her direction, urging his mount forward so that his horse was nose-to-nose with hers. 'Is this little divergence from the trail all for my benefit, perchance?'

'Don't flatter yourself,' she muttered, her expression still deceptively serene. 'Still, you don't appear to be a very strong rider. We wouldn't want you to sustain an injury.'

'Wouldn't you?' he asked.

'Certainly not, Señor San Nicolau. This is your first trip to our beautiful kingdom, after all. There shall be no injuries or disappearances on my watch.'

It took most of his effort not to laugh at the saccharine sweetness of her voice, shocked that no one else could see the barely restrained malice in the golden-brown gaze directed upon him. If she wanted to challenge him, he would not back down. To his surprise, most of their small group of guests, including the formidable Prince Lorenz, soon decided to turn back to the smoother path, led by Beatriz. The Frenchman paused for a long moment, looking forlornly back and forth between the two parties, and then quickly came to the same decision.

'We will meet you down at the lake,' Minerva called to her friend, then swiftly turned and nudged her horse on at a remarkably faster pace than before.

They continued downhill, dodging tree branches and underbrush, Liro's heartbeat increasing at every possible misstep, but quite impressed at Strawberry's agility. He could not take credit himself, for the horse seemed to instinctively know where to step and where to slow down slightly, but his tolerance was tested significantly when the Irish man nudged himself forward, overtaking him. Seemingly gathering even more speed and bravery, the fool began to show off, overtaking Minerva and disappearing into the distance as he showed off his impressive horsemanship.

'Isn't he going a little fast?' Liro called out, just close enough that she could hear him. She didn't answer so he continued to ramble loudly, 'I suppose we will know soon enough if we find his body at the bottom of a cliff further down.'

Silence.

'I suppose you would rather it be me than him,'

Liro pondered loudly. 'Wouldn't want to sacrifice one of your eligible bachelors.'

Minerva paused her mount, looking back over her shoulder at him. 'You talk a lot more these days. It's quite annoying.'

Liro hid a smile behind his hand. 'Out of interest…which of the three charming fellows is in the lead so far?'

'Just three?' she answered easily. 'You removed yourself from the running so quickly?'

'Darling, we both know that I am in a whole other league.'

The ghost of a smile hinted at the corners of her lips now, but she turned away from him, holding herself at that maddening distance he knew he deserved. She was being sensible, behaving rationally. He was the one who seemed unable to toe the line. He was the one who had insisted upon staying here, appointing himself some kind of unofficial royal investigator of sorts, when it was clear he was unwelcome.

Was he trying to perform a penance for having left things so badly between them? Or did his motives run deeper than that, to a place he had long refused to look at or entertain?

'Why are you still here, Liro?' She exhaled on a long sigh as they began moving downhill through the forest once more.

'I'm a businessman. I'm here to hunt down a new deal.'

'We both know that Arqaleta plays no role in your area of business.'

Liro paused, processing the fact that his hunch was right, and the royal family had not been consulted on this potentially large change to their kingdom's economy. 'Perhaps I'm just curious to know why a woman who remained comfortably single for the past fourteen years seems set to choose a husband based upon a week of courtship.'

'From the way you asked that question, I gather that you already know the answer.' Minerva shifted atop her saddle, pushing an errant strand of hair away from her face. 'I've had some bad press, but I always knew that the time would come for me to marry. And I have decided to solve that problem now rather than waiting until later.'

'So this is what *you* want?' he asked, needing to hear her say it with her own mouth.

'I'm the Crown Princess. It's what is required of me, in order to maintain the future of my kingdom, so of *course* it is what I want.'

'What a perfectly rehearsed response, Your Highness,' he said, feeling irritation rise in his throat. Of course, there had to be a more pressing reason why she had decided to marry so suddenly, but she was hardly going to divulge that to him of all people.

Silence fell between them as the trail became more demanding and he found himself entranced by her skill and followed her lead. When he performed a small jump over a creek without comment, he found her waiting for him, her gaze narrowed and watchful.

'You remembered some of my lessons, then.'

He smiled, remembering how she had forced him to practise his horsemanship once she'd figured out he was utterly terrified. His father had been a champion polo player in his youth, forcing the sport onto each of his sons. His older brothers had taken to the sport naturally, whereas Liro...had not. After a series of gruelling lessons and bad falls as a young boy, he'd instantly begun to have nightmares. His mother, a terrified rider herself, had taken to shielding him from the pressure, bringing him along with her to the library or the town fun fair when his brothers were at matches. His father hadn't resumed his pressure after her death, instead shifting to the outright mocking and derision of his sensitive youngest son.

'Your teaching methods were impatient but effective.' He moved his mare alongside hers, close enough that he could smell the delicious scent of coconut from the styling oil she had always loved so much. 'You were just as intent upon ignoring me then as you are now.'

'Says the guy who barely spoke to me for the first four years.'

'I barely spoke to anyone, not just you.' He shook off the discomfort at her reminder of his youth. As he had been a skinny, awkward teen in a family of much bigger and louder men, his father and brothers had often taken enjoyment in commenting on his uselessness. Perhaps that was why, when he'd been sent to Arqaleta with the oddly specific purpose of befriending the princess, he had taken it as an opportunity to show his worth.

She was right—that first summer, he'd hardly uttered a single word in her presence. He had always struggled socially and tended towards self-isolation, but around Minerva he'd been speechless for an entirely different reason. From the first moment he'd seen her, she'd made him feel uncomfortably seen. Her wide golden-brown eyes and open, friendly manner had made him feel as though he were staring at the sun for the first time after years spent in the dark. Add the fact she'd been the most beautiful girl he had ever laid his eyes on...

'I looked forward to coming here every summer. Being here, getting over my fear of riding, I was happy. Despite my silence.' He surprised himself with his honesty, knowing that she could simply wave him off and go right back to ignoring him all over again. But whatever part of him that had forced him to keep his yacht moored in the harbour last night was still very much in control, and it desperately needed her to know the important part she'd played in his life.

'Your silence was just you, Liro. Besides, I talked enough for both of us.' Her voice trailed off and he wondered if she was thinking about all the things

she'd said when she'd thought he was ignoring her.
Her sadness about her father, her worries about becoming queen one day. He had listened to every
word, storing away each detail and wondering how
he might help. He wondered who she talked to now—
probably Bea or her mother. He wondered if they let
her talk things out all by herself, as she needed to, or
if they jumped in with suggestions, tangling her up.
Maybe that was how she had wound up in this ridiculous week of marital matchmaking with strangers.

He let her stew over whatever thoughts were pil-
ing up in her mind, understanding that he was no
longer one of her confidants. He had walked away
from that position the moment he'd chosen to leave
Arqaleta on a ship in the dead of night, like a coward.

There was no audience here as he kept pace perfectly behind her, no one to play nice in front of. He
relaxed back and allowed his horse to navigate the
rocky path down the mountain, enjoying the view,
the rolling hills and the smell of the sea air in the
distance.

But mostly he enjoyed looking at Minerva, the
sweat just barely evident on her brow as she held
her reins. She rode so effortlessly, with such smooth,
subtle movements of her hips and thighs… It mes-
merised him.

It had been far too long since he'd last indulged in
any kind of sexual gratification with anything other
than his own hand. He'd thought of her last night,

after that kiss… He'd brought himself to the swiftest release of his life in a brief moment of weakness, accessing the memories of the brief few weeks he'd had her in his arms he'd stored away. He was so focused upon curbing his illicit thoughts that he was not prepared when the tree line broke and the ferocious midday sun blinded him momentarily.

'Be careful!' Her voice called out to him from a few feet to his left, where the path took a sudden, sharp turn. He pulled the reins hard, trying to get the horse to stop. By the time his eyes adjusted and he realised that he had veered close to the edge of a rocky cliff, there was little that he could do, only pull the reins harder, feeling the horse's hooves skid beneath him as the old girl tried to stop. He was aware of the sound of galloping and the sound of a shout before the sky tilted and he was thrown heavily backwards.

# CHAPTER FOUR

THE WHOLE THING happened in slow motion. Minerva could do nothing but watch as Liro pulled too hard on his reins, startled by the sudden cliff drop-off that lay in front of them. The sun had blinded him momentarily but now his eyes were wide, darting towards her with realisation, right as his horse reared up and sent his body tumbling backwards towards the drop. He landed with a sickening thud upon the ground.

The horse skidded to a stop a few feet away, thankfully avoiding trampling him or more danger. But, as Minerva jumped down from her own horse, she felt real fear rise like bile in her throat. She had done this—she had brought him down this path, knowing that he was not a strong rider. She'd told him she wanted him gone, and in that moment it had felt painfully true, but that did not mean she actually wished him harm.

Liro looked past her, his face paling as he looked upon the edge of the cliff. In an impressive display of nonchalance, he slid himself a few inches away from the precipice before flopping back to the ground with a grunt.

'Are you okay?' Minerva breathed, falling down to her knees beside him. His small movements indicated a lack of serious injury, but one could never be sure. She'd been there on the awful day when the stable master's daughter had been thrown from a temperamental horse. She would never forget the horror of it. Minerva had been by Bea's side every step of the way as she'd recovered from a serious spinal injury and the event had wound up bonding them as friends for life. Again, she cursed herself for being so petty and impulsive in bringing Liro down such a demanding trail and risking his safety this way.

'I'm fine.' He heaved himself up onto his elbows, his muscles straining against the dust-covered sleeves of his jacket. He grimaced as he tried to straighten further.

'You're hurt.' She flattened her hand against his chest to hold him still.

He looked up at her, stormy eyes glowing more green than grey today, obscenely ethereal in the sunlight. Eyes should not be such an unpredictable colour, she reasoned briefly, trying not to focus on the steady heat of his chest rising and falling under her explorative touch. She pressed his ribs slightly, watching his face for signs of pain.

'Surely the objective of taking me down this path

was to allow me to fall to my death?' he asked, then immediately groaned as she increased the pressure of her touch.

'I want you gone, not dead.' She growled. 'Stop talking for a moment and catch your breath you… you little fool.' She cursed under her breath, holding his shoulder to force him still. He obeyed, his breaths coming shallow and hard as he lay flat on the ground. She took the opportunity to lift up his shirt to ensure there weren't any ribs poking out, causing his breathlessness. No protruding bones greeted her, only rock-hard abs.

'Little…fool?' he repeated.

She could hear the hint of a smirk in his voice and fought not to laugh, if only to break the terror of the past couple of minutes. 'I don't know…it just came out.'

'I thought that phrase was reserved for waifish heroines in period dramas. Do you think of me as a dainty damsel you've had to rescue?'

'I don't think of you at all.' She felt his eyes on her but refused to look at him as she stood up and smacked the dust roughly from her knees. 'Or at least I didn't, until you reappeared without any explanation, seemingly hell-bent on derailing my life at every turn.'

A heavy silence fell between them but she refused to apologise when she spoke the truth. Well, not about not thinking of him…of course that part was a bare-faced lie…but the rest of it. She had been on the verge of tears all morning then had been forced to put on her best performance during this ridiculous ride, only to have him bring up the past and question her choices.

She looked over to where his previously spooked mare was gazing peacefully near a tree, and felt a shiver course through her again at how close he'd come to injury. She should offer to help him up, she realised, but her body felt frozen in place. Everything about the past twenty-four hours was just too much.

If only Liro had just left again. If only he had never returned in the first place, like her father had done all those years ago. It was the one gift he'd given them, that clean break. It was far easier to forget someone when you could pretend they didn't exist. Having Liro here now made her feel as if all of her work in putting herself back together had been for nothing—as if just looking at him made her hurt all over again.

She had made her plans for this week and the months that would follow as she finally stepped into her role as Queen of Arqaleta. She refused to let the reappearance of one insufferable man throw everything off kilter.

His expression became gravely serious. 'Minerva…when I left…'

'I have no wish to discuss the past any more,' she said quickly, feeling a hint of panic creep into her voice. 'Once some time had passed, I realised that you breaking our betrothal was the best possible outcome for us both. I travelled the world and lived out my dream in a way I never could have if we had been forced into a marriage of convenience.'

'So you're done living your dreams, just like that?' he asked. 'Do you truly believe that any of these suitors will satisfy you?'

She froze at his cruel words, at how close they came to getting right under her skin. 'Is this the only reason you came back here? To question my choices?'

'Maybe I'm just here to try to make amends to someone I hurt. Someone I once considered a friend.'

She shook her head, hurt climbing her throat as she looked down at him where he still lay at her feet. 'Well, Liro, you're around fourteen years too late.'

The sound of hooves coming closer from a distance was a welcome distraction from how deep into unwelcome territory their conversation had got. By the time John's horse appeared from around the bend, Liro had sprung easily up to his feet.

'Everything all right?' the Irishman asked, his eyes darting shrewdly between them, as though he feared he'd made a gross miscalculation in trying to show off his horsemanship.

'The mare became spooked by the drop and threw her rider,' Minerva replied coolly. 'Thankfully Señor San Nicolau was not hurt.'

If Liro was surprised at her effort to spare him any embarrassment, he restrained himself from commenting. Instead, he focused on putting on the bravest face to belie the obvious bruising he'd endured from his fall. He walked over to his horse and swung up with only the tiniest groan under his breath, which he quickly disguised with a cough.

Minerva smiled behind the cover of her own stallion's flank as she pretended to tighten the saddle. For all he had insisted that the prince she'd known was dead and gone, this hint of vulnerability was something he couldn't help but show. She thought of the first few summers they'd been forced together, when she'd helped him get over his fear of horse riding, and he'd helped her with the remedial schoolwork she had been trying to catch up on for ever. They hadn't been close friends, but they'd never been enemies.

As they rode back towards the lake to meet up with the others, Minerva couldn't help but watch Liro closely for any other signs of pain. He remained silent, not speaking another word until he bid them goodbye at the stables and disappeared in the direction of the harbour. Stubborn man, she grumbled to herself as she was once again danced with attention by Jean-Claude and Prince Lorenz.

Prince Oliveiro might have adopted a new name and look, but when it came to hiding himself away without further explanation it seemed he hadn't changed so much.

\* \* \*

Liro did not return for the informal dinner her mother hosted that evening, nor was he present at breakfast the next morning. Minerva resisted the urge to go down to the harbour to see if his ridiculously oversized yacht was still moored there, as a light fog had obstructed her view from her bedroom window the night before. Thankfully she had managed to fall into an exhausted sleep after the previous afternoon's horse-riding adventure had turned into an impromptu rowing lesson from Prince Lorenz on the lake. She had been surprised by his astute conversation and dry wit, and had vowed to give him an honest chance after his poor first impression.

But still Liro's voice was in her head far too often, asking her why now? Why the rush? He had got under her skin simply by reappearing in her life and then he had had the audacity to question her as well. His inquisition had only served to reaffirm her effort to get to know each of her three choices of potential husband. They truly were expert choices, showing her that her mother knew her better than she probably even knew herself.

The agenda for Wednesday began with an exhibition at their museum of cultural history in Albo's historical town square, one of her favourite places in all of Arqaleta. The curator had gathered and assembled an interactive exhibit of Arqaleta's rich history of weaponry, including their world-famous bow and arrow collections.

Minerva stood by her mother's side as the Queen gave a beautiful speech about the history of their beautiful island kingdom, a speech that Minerva knew came from the heart. Crowds had gathered, filling up their modest town square and spilling over into the surrounding streets. Street vendors sold sweet treats and their world-famous Arqaletan pastry, the honeybee, on every corner. The scent of warm honey and crisp, flaking pastry filled the air and made her mouth water.

She hadn't eaten much at breakfast, and would have loved nothing more than to cross the street and grab one for herself, but duty called. Still, her stomach rumbled as she gazed longingly in the direction of a young couple sharing a crisp, golden honeybee between them.

'Hungry?'

A low voice came from behind her shoulder. She turned sharply to find Liro, looking relaxed and pensive. How long had he been standing there? He was dressed in a fine navy suit today, his rich red waves smoothed back in a classic style that emphasised his strong nose and cheekbones. He had never been conventionally attractive as a teen, but every time she laid eyes on him now she found herself stricken anew by what a presence he made. He made no effort to hide his tattoos today, letting the curling black lines snake up from his open collar. She still couldn't make out what they were…a forest of some sort? An animal?

He noticed her staring and she turned away quickly away. Her mother's speech had ended, but the curator was talking through his inspiration for the exhibit now, and she had not been paying attention.

'You seem tense, *princesa*. Is selecting your favourite suitor from the bachelor buffet proving more difficult than you'd hoped?' He moved to stand by her side, using the handkerchief from his breast pocket to idly polish the sunglasses in his hands.

'You're still here.' She feigned complete boredom, focusing her attention fully upon the display. 'When you disappeared again, I thought yesterday had finally convinced you to move on.'

'And miss finding out who your beloved new king consort will be?' He clucked his tongue. 'Not a chance.'

His handsome smirk sent a shiver along her skin and she resisted the urge to walk away, to leave him standing there alone. *Bachelor buffet…* Her mind whirled with discomfort at his words, the blunt reminder of the choice she had to make soon. They had an audience, she was a princess and princesses had rules. A princess did not cut people off, and she definitely did not stick her tongue out at them for good measure.

She settled upon turning her head politely to feign

interest in the curator's speech, listening to the older man wax lyrical about primitive arrows and the very first cannon.

The heat was growing stronger by the minute and her stomach continued to growl softly as she put her best effort into appearing utterly engrossed. When the speech finally ended, she resisted the urge to sigh, knowing that now she would be forced to walk at a snail's pace around the exhibit when really all she wanted was to go straight to the bow and arrow section and see which pieces had been chosen.

The scent of melted sugar and butter teased her nostrils, seeming to have wafted across to her on a cruel breeze. But then by some miracle a pastry appeared in her vision, wrapped in a delicate white napkin in Liro's large, callused hand.

'A gift from an admirer, Your Highness,' he said, placing the delicious pastry in her hands before she could say no.

He watched her, eyes sparkling with sin, urging her to cause a scene and refuse his gift. He had clearly been standing nearby for long enough to notice her gazing over at the food and he had gone and got one for her.

That realisation shouldn't have sent a glittering shimmer of warmth running through her, but food had always been her weakness. She was utterly ravenous, and the honeybee was her absolute favourite out of all the pastries he could have chosen. She bowed her head in the direction of the vendor, who smiled and gestured towards her excitedly. A queue had already begun to form around his stall now that the people could see the princess holding one of his perfectly baked confections.

'Consider it a peace offering,' Liro said. 'You could have left me in the dirt, or at the very least you could have told the embarrassing truth of what happened, rather than preserve the dignity of a *little fool*.'

His reminder of her phrase made a sudden snort of laughter escape her. She tried to hold it in, but it was too late, and a second bubble of mirth followed the first. Liro's eyes seemed to glitter with victory at the sound, making her wish he would put back on his sunglasses. He was…too much…and once again he was distracting her from her duty.

Sighing with defeat, she bit ceremoniously into a small corner of the pastry in the hope it would send him away. She was not prepared for the sheer perfection of flavour that met her taste buds. All royal teachings abandoned, she proceeded to finish the entire thing in less than three bites. She looked down at the napkin, filled with nothing but crumbs, and realised her lapse of propriety.

Liro leaned in, a smile on his lips. 'Don't worry, everyone is far too busy looking at your museum curator struggling to lift a bow to notice you inhaling a glorified croissant.'

'*He's* doing the demonstration?' She looked up, sure enough seeing the elderly curator lifting an ancient bow from its case. Her fingers itched with longing.

'Strange that they would choose an elderly academic when they have a world-famous Olympic archer sitting right here,' he mused. 'Or is this part of that new traditional image I've heard of?'

'I don't always have to take the spotlight.' She shrugged.

The look Liro gave her was one of complete disbelief. 'Your experience as an athlete on the global stage is a huge advantage. Teenagers had posters of you on their walls, for goodness' sake. Maybe they fear your power and influence.'

The crowd began to cheer around them as the elderly curator hit a weak arrow in the vague direction of the target. It was an utterly pathetic shot, but still she applauded. Heaven forbid anyone wound an old man's pride.

But still, as the display ended and the bell was called for the sit-down luncheon inside, Liro's words resounded in her mind. *Maybe they fear your power and influence.* Of course, she knew that her position as a female leader in a kingdom traditionally ruled by men was fraught with issues. Her own mother had hit many roadblocks in her reign, but she was confident that she knew which battles to fight and which to cede. Or at least, that was what she had been telling herself.

When they were seated, she watched from afar as Liro conversed easily among the guests at his table on the far side of the room. She felt his attention upon her at regular intervals and noticed his eyes narrow when the band started up and Prince Lorenz, John and Jean-Claude each appeared to ask her to dance. She indulged Jean-Claude first, laughing as she attempted to teach him a traditional Arqaletan slow dance. John stepped up for the next song, impressing her with his speed and agility as he led the dance. All the while, it took far too much of her focus not to let her eyes wander to the brooding red-haired hulk at the edge of the room.

It was on her third turn around the room, with Prince Lorenz this time, that she allowed herself to take a quick look—only to find his table empty. She craned her neck, looking around the hall, finally spying him standing in the far corner of the room with a familiar silver-haired politician, Robart. Minerva frowned as the two men shook hands, looking very chummy for brand-new acquaintances. Confirming her suspicions, Liro took out his phone and showed Robart something, earning a wink from the older man and a clap on the back.

When Liro looked up at her, she saw guilt cross his features and felt her stomach tighten. Her suspicions had been based only on a hunch, but one look in his eyes and she knew she had been right. He'd come here to conquer, to seize control in the shadows, just as his father had tried to do all those years ago.

The song stopped and she thanked her lucky stars. Prince Lorenz was a wonderful dancer, but he talked non-stop, and she just needed to breathe a moment alone. Something small and fragile ached in her chest, but she managed to maintain her composure as she walked past the tables filled with guests, up the grand staircase and out towards the rest rooms. Only at the very last moment did she realise she had changed her course and had slipped over the velvet ropes that led to the darkened display halls.

Automatic lights clicked on above her head as her heels clicked on the floors, the musty scent of wood polish reminding her of childhood visits here with her father. He had been an amateur archer himself, one of the only things they'd ever had in common. Her natural skill at the sport had never been enough to capture his attention, but still, she had him to thank for the introduction. It was woven into the very history of their country, in the talented bow-makers and fletchers for which Arqaleta had long been world renowned.

She came to a stop in front of a vast case filled with wooden longbows and bronze-tipped arrows, blinking at the faint reflection of herself in the glass. Another tiara adorned her head today, a small piece that had been designed to commemorate her Olympic gold medal. It was an accomplishment that many members of parliament had initially been against her seeking, deeming it unroyal and too time consuming. Robart had been one of the loudest voices against her suitability as future queen, so it stung to see Liro shaking the man's hand.

She didn't know how long she stood there in silence. When the sound of heavy footsteps approached slowly from the hallway, she didn't need to look up. Just as when they'd been young and she'd tried to avoid him, Liro always found her.

'Hiding from your duty, Min…?' He tutted, his hands deep in his pockets as he came to a stop by her side. 'Your handsome bachelors will grow restless.'

'I'm surprised you noticed, with how cosy you seemed with Robart.' She laced her tone with saccharine sweetness, her words echoing off the high glass ceiling above them. 'Tell me…you're not trying to push your way into the harbour rezoning proposals by any chance, are you? The ones that my mother refused to sign? Would that be the reason you've refused to leave my kingdom for the past three days?'

Liro looked down at her, his stern expression breaking slightly. 'You already know about the harbour project?'

'People assume that, because I have stopped pushing the boundaries and chosen to step into my role fully, I have somehow stopped being the most focused person in the room.' She met his eyes, anger masking the strange sadness in her chest at the confirmation that she was right. That he had been toying with her these past couple of days, biding his time as he tried to close a deal.

Liro hadn't noticed Minerva leave the museum's function area at first, having been waylaid in conversation by that insufferable politician. Once he'd realised she'd gone, and noticed the distinct absence of the tall, dark and handsome Prince Lorenz, he'd made quick work of stalking down every exhibit hall until he found her.

Now here they were, arguing again. But this time about something he honestly had not intended to keep from her. They'd just been rather busy kissing, arguing and avoiding death by cliff-fall thus far. He took in the molten bronze ire in her gaze and shook off an inappropriate thrum of desire. Now was certainly not the time, not when he had myriad things to explain to her about his intentions with the development plans.

She raised a hand to stop him before he could say a single word. 'Save it. I knew about that project from the moment whispers began to circulate. I haven't raised my concerns because I don't have any.'

'You…don't intend to stop it?'

'My mother and I have very different views on what progress looks like. I believe that rigid control breeds secrecy and corruption, whereas compromise and fairness lead to more balanced results. I want Arqaleta to grow, and growth hurts sometimes, to lead to better things.'

He stared at her for a long moment, before he heard himself murmur. 'You're going to make an amazing queen.'

She turned from him, hiding her face. 'There is no need for you to continue attending events and stalking me for pretence, Liro. Finish your deal and go.'

He took in the rigid pose and the guarded look in her eyes and realised she believed he'd been using their past as a cover, to hide his dealings. If only that were the truth. He took a step towards her, irritation flaring as she took an equal step back. She wanted to keep herself at a distance while they had this conversation but…oh…that just wasn't going to work for him. He kept moving forward until she looked up at him with some of that glorious fury. He wanted her anger; he needed it, all of a sudden.

'That deal may be why I accepted the invitation, Minerva…but I think it's damned obvious to both of us that it is not why I stayed.' He stepped closer again, crowding her against the smooth glass of a display case.

'If you truly considered yourself a friend to me, Liro, you'd leave.'

'If I was your friend, I would tell you that you

don't actually want to marry any of them. They won't make you happy.'

'That's rich, coming from you.' She stiffened, holding herself at a distance. 'I don't want a happy-ever-after, just a husband. The kingdom's tradition has always included a king consort and I won't be the one to break that.'

'Tell me what you need, Min,' he urged, moving close enough that their chests almost touched. 'When is the last time anyone bothered to ask?'

'Right now? I need to go back to the party.'

'Stay,' he said, softly enough for it to seem like a request. But the very idea of allowing her to run back to those preening fools, of continuing to watch from afar as they salivated and fought over her attentions like pups… His fists clenched involuntarily. She needed to be cared for in a way that no one else seemed able to see. She was so wound up, so tense and close to breaking point, he feared she might shatter. She put everyone else's expectations ahead of her own, living each day for her precious duty. Had she ever known a single day of true freedom?

'I should reveal your identity right here and now in front of everyone,' she whispered, her breath close enough to fan against his lips. 'I should have done it the moment I first recognised you.'

'You didn't, though. You were far too busy kissing me.' He tilted his head closer, caging her body in softly with his arms. Despite her threats, she hadn't made a single move to leave. A fact that made all of the blood in his body rush below his belt. 'I think you know what you need, Minerva. I think that's part of the reason why you're so determined to tear strips off me every time we get too close. We both have a lot of pent-up emotions that we didn't get the chance to work out.'

'Are you about to suggest that I hop into bed with you one more time for closure? Bang it out of our systems?' She scoffed, but he could see the way her honey-brown eyes tried to hide flickers of desire.

'I've wondered if one night of having you back in my bed would be enough. Wondered if it would make this burning need go away…or would it only stoke us back into a full-blown forest fire?'

He leaned forward, lifting her hand to press the ghost of a kiss against the inside of her wrist. She sighed and he felt it like a punch to the gut. He was so hard, he could barely think, but she needed to come to him the rest of the way. She needed to admit that what he was saying was the truth and that there was only one logical way for them to work this tension out and move on.

Because he knew that was all it could be—they both did.

'Tell me you haven't thought about it, Min,' he murmured softly, inching a second kiss upon her palm. 'Tell me that you haven't fantasised about me when your day is done and you're all alone in that big bed of yours. Tell me to leave you alone…and I'll go.'

His own needy words shocked him, an uncomfortable echo of his younger self that took him by surprise. He wasn't usually so unguarded with a woman. On the occasions he bothered to seek out company at port, he kept things brief. He treated his sex life much the same as his appearances in the board room—calm, rare and to the point.

But here…in this dimly lit, echoing museum hall as he waited for her to speak…he didn't feel calm at all. She reached up, placing a hand upon his chest, and for a moment he thought she might push him away. But she didn't. She left it there, a single maddening point of contact between them.

'I've thought about you,' she said quietly, closing her eyes tightly.

And there it was. He closed his eyes, taking in a single shuddering breath as his body strained hard against the seam of his fanciest dress trousers. When he opened his eyes again, she was watching him.

'Why am I telling you these things?' she whispered, sliding her hands up to his shoulders. Her fingers flexed upon his muscles and he flexed back shamelessly. Her slow smile was just a little shy and filled with the evidence of her desire.

'You don't want to be left alone, that's why.'

She bit on her lower lip. 'I don't know what I want. Not when it comes to you.'

He knew how easy it would be to lean forward and close the distance between them, to quiet her indecision with kisses. He wouldn't hold back; he'd instantly begin to show her exactly what he would do if she ever came back to his bed. One night with the woman who had haunted him…. One night to lay to rest all of the foolish memories he could never shake… He wanted it so badly his fingers shook and his throat ran dry. So why then did he find himself taking a step backwards?

What did he plan to do, undress her here on the cold stone floor then disappear off to sea once again? Another final memory to keep, because that had worked so well last time, hadn't it?

Liro cleared his throat, looking back towards the exit. She was a crown princess with a museum full of people waiting for her to return; they could be found at any moment. She had so many people pushing her to comply with their needs, taking her kindness, using her.

She leaned towards him for a split second, a single glimpse of confusion in her eyes that she quickly covered up as she too seemed to come to her senses. Standing up straight, she pushed past him and walked away a few steps. She paused under an archway, flanked by two statues in gleaming golden armour.

'You said you'd go, if I told you one more time,' she said, her words echoing, cold and unyielding, in the cavernous hall.

Silence stretched between them. He knew what he had said and knew that it was the best course of action. But still, something within him growled in protest as she walked away.

# CHAPTER FIVE

MINERVA RETURNED TO the function and threw herself into princess mode, speaking with everyone who sought out her attention and dancing until her feet ached. She didn't see Liro again. By the time the event wound down and she had returned to the palace, she was exhausted enough to fall into a dreamless sleep.

The next morning was a day filled with events, starting with a beautiful folk concert and poetry reading at the children's hospital. She resisted the urge to check if a certain giant black yacht had departed the kingdom yet, just as she resisted scanning the shoreline for it as her car drove past the marina. This week was about securing her path to the crown, not ruminating over the past like a moody teenager. She was good at compartmentalising her emotions. In a job where she was expected to be *on* at all times in public, she had to be.

Still, she couldn't stop herself from looking over

her shoulder countless times throughout the long morning, and even longer afternoon, wondering if she might find a familiar pair of green-grey eyes watching her.

The sun was low in the sky when she and her mother were deposited at the bottom of the steps of the palace, but the idea of going inside and beginning her preparations for the evening's charity auction made her feel strangely empty. It would be a wonderful event, with all proceeds going towards so many causes close to her heart. But the idea of spending more time with John, Prince Lorenz and Jean-Claude made her feel utterly exhausted. She knew she had to begin to make her decision soon, before Mama's announcement. But all of her cool-headed determination from the past few weeks of preparation had begun to wane slightly, leaving her more than a little unsure of her decision to rush into a royal marriage of convenience.

She felt her mother's eyes on her as they walked along the corridor towards the family suites. Before she reached the privacy of her room, her mother pulled her away towards a quiet corner of the garden. 'Have any of the candidates I invited caught your eye yet?'

'I have it narrowed down to three.' She listed off the names of the men she'd chosen and saw a strange look cross her mother's features. 'What, you disagree?'

'Not at all, darling,' Mama said quickly. 'You

asked me to send the invitations—the rest is entirely up to you. But...none of the others caught your attention?'

After a moment of hesitation, Minerva knew that her only choice was to lie and change the topic to the speech they'd been preparing for the announcement on Saturday. Her mother continued to look at her a little too closely, a fact that did nothing for the nervous energy that had plagued her since that moment in the museum hall yesterday afternoon.

When her mother finally excused herself to begin to get ready, Minerva knew she should follow along. She didn't have much time before the stylists and make-up artists arrived to do a quick change from her day look to evening formal.

The scent of citrus filled the air, floating over from the large glass conservatory hall where tonight's event would take place. She ambled towards her bedroom door, hesitating at the last moment. In the absence of her beloved sport, her thoughts had become increasingly tangled and harder to manage over the past few months. Time in the archery arena was time that she would usually have spent thinking about and working through the things that weighed upon her mind. But there was one place in the palace grounds that had always given her peace...

A hum of nervous energy seemed to zing through her at the idea, and before she knew it she had veered through an archway and was quietly cutting across the gardens in her polished ivory day dress. Her security team had remained in the upper hallway: the palace grounds were safe enough for her to wander a little. She would not be gone long; she just needed some time alone to breathe.

Minerva knew where she was heading instinctively, even before the tell-tale scent of moss hit her nostrils. She hadn't come down to their old lakeside haunt in many years. She had thought she had prepared well enough for the energy required to get through such a high intensity week of events, but nothing could have prepared her for him. He'd plied her with croissants, asked her for her secrets and cracked open all the tightly controlled longing she'd kept hidden away.

Three days ago, she had been fine. She had been more than fine: she had been *quite* content with the prospect of selecting a husband. Then he'd reappeared in her world with all the subtlety of an atomic bomb, making her question everything…planting seeds of rebellion, just as he had all those years ago.

Well, she was not the same girl he had used and discarded at nineteen, and it was high time he understood that. If he turned up at the auction tonight, she would give him a piece of her mind. She would tell him exactly how she felt, no punches pulled.

The stone archway was mostly covered in leaves and branches, and a wave of sadness came over her as she fought her way through the tree-covered pathway. The secret lake was still there, and blessedly not completely overgrown with foliage. The stone statues lay sleeping, as though they had been waiting for her return. She ran her fingers along the graceful neck of a marble swan, trying to adjust her eyes to the much softer light.

She didn't see the broad figure that lay in wait upon one of the stone benches, inhaling sharply when he stood and revealed himself.

'What are you doing here?'

'Probably the same thing that you are,' Liro answered, his expression more guarded than she had ever seen. 'I thought I would visit this place…before I leave.'

'And when will that be?' she asked, trying to hide how shaken she felt at the sight of seeing him here…in *their* place. They hadn't been here since that very last night when everything had fallen apart. The thought of being a royal bride had felt so exciting back then, while now she looked upon it as just another task she had to tick off in order to perform the job she had been raised to do.

'I'm leaving tonight,' he said. 'I had debated attending the charity auction, considering that I had already purchased my ticket, but I am sure the funds will still make it to the right places in my absence.'

Silence fell between them, along with a million unspoken words that Minerva wanted to say. Angry words, questions and above all longing. She wanted to tell him exactly how she had felt when he'd left, exactly how much his absence had shaped her as a person.

'I won't be backing down from my bid on the harbour expansion. But I have decided that I will not be personally overseeing the rest of the negotiations myself.'

He paused for a long moment before taking a step towards her. 'Everything I said yesterday was the truth, but I see now that it was unfair to return here. You've made it clear that my presence is unwelcome and…despite what you may think… I never set out to upset you, Minerva.'

She thought of the things he'd said in that darkened museum hall and felt heat blaze along her skin. *Tell me that you haven't fantasised about me*, he'd urged. *Tell me to leave you alone…* She hadn't been able to say either of those things with confidence.

The truth was she had fantasised about him more times than she could count. Just this morning she had awoken swollen and slick with longing, imagining his strong, capable hands doing truly delicious things to her. She'd only barely resisted calling out his name as she'd brought herself to climax, then had instantly felt raw and embarrassed afterwards as she got ready to go about her day.

'You said…' She inhaled a deep breath, nerves and indecision making it catch in her throat. 'You said that we both know why you stayed. I want you to tell me.'

'I stayed for you, Min,' he said easily. 'I stayed because, once I saw you again, I couldn't quite seem to leave.'

She took a step towards him. 'But you will leave. If I tell you to.'

'If that's what you want, then yes.'

Was that what she wanted? For days now she had told herself that she wanted Liro to disappear, along with all the complicated emotions that seemed to bubble up in his presence. She had been so consumed with holding herself together, with focusing on the celebrations and the matchmaking...

*Tell me what you need, Min. When was the last time anyone asked?*

She needed to kiss him. She needed it so badly, her hands trembled with the effort of remaining at a distance. Just once, she promised herself. One last kiss to get the closure she'd been denied fourteen years ago. She could see his fingers flexing by his sides. He wanted to touch her...and she wanted so badly to be touched. Before she could over-think, she closed the remaining distance between them. There were so many things she wanted to say, but words failed her as she reached for him, leaning into his warmth.

Her lips found his as though they had always known this was where she would end up. As though that very first kiss after she'd recognised him had simply been an appetiser, an initial spark of kindling upon the embers of their past. She had been smouldering for him for days now—she could deny it no longer. And, when his hands sank into her hair, she groaned against his mouth with relief.

'This…' she murmured as she paused for a breath. 'This is what I need from you.'

A growl came from somewhere low in his throat as he pulled her closer so that another inch of space was removed between them.

'If this is what you need from me, princess,' he urged, thrusting his hardness against her thigh. 'Then use me.'

His words felt wrong, somehow… But his tone was erotic and dominating so she let him take control for a moment, pushing her back against the tree trunk.

'You missed me.' His words were a statement rather than a question and she didn't have the energy to rebuke them as a shiver passed through her and reality began to encroach upon this tiny oasis of pleasure.

'I missed *this*,' she corrected, not able to give him any more than that. She'd gone so long without true connection to another and she was powerless to stop. They kissed until her back ached against the rough tree but, every time she told herself that it was time to leave, she didn't. In the end it was he who pulled back first, his eyes never leaving hers as he caught his breath.

'You make me feel like a teenager.' He growled, a subtle smirk on his lips as he traced the pad of his index finger down the side of her neck and along one collar bone.

His touch was feather-light and almost tender, confusing her even more. She didn't want softness from him. It was too much and yet entirely not enough. She pushed gently until she could slide away from the tree, needing to breathe.

'Your compliments are good for a girl's confidence.' She aimed for a light tone, failing miserably. 'Y-you've got better at kissing since then.'

Liro's voice was silky as sin as he replied, 'I've had a lot of time to think about it.'

This man… Minerva inhaled a deep breath, trying to cool off the instant heat that rushed through her body with his words. She knew that staying here and talking like this with him was dangerous. She knew it, and still she met his eyes with a direct challenge. 'I think sometimes time tends to embellish certain memories to make them seem better than they actually were.'

His eyes lowered to her lips. 'Well…there's only one way to know for sure.'

She didn't know who kissed whom first this time, not that it mattered anyway. The space between them was instantly gone and his lips were crushed against hers, his hands in her hair holding her just where he wanted her. Her body sang at his touch, a shiver of awareness spreading along the skin of her nape and down her spine like wildfire. The crackling heat of the flame finally being ignited between them was stifling. All rational thought of this being wrong was utterly consumed by a hunger so intense it took her breath away. She felt his hands tightening on her waist, pulling her closely against him so that she could feel the evidence of his arousal pressing against her lower abdomen.

God, how she had missed this feeling. She remembered once telling him that the intensity of her desire for him scared her. She had been younger then, a curious girl entering into her first passionate love affair. He had been inexperienced too, but had still always behaved like a gentleman. He'd held off on his own desires to make sure that she was ready before they took their relationship to the next level.

She was not a virgin now. Nor was he feeling particularly gentlemanly, judging by the way he pushed her back against the tree while his fingers frantically worked at the delicate pearl buttons at her throat. The front of her dress came open slowly, her simple cotton bra revealed to him inch by inch. His big hands splayed over the soft material, rubbing against her tautened nipples through the thin barrier. She sighed at the contact, fighting the urge to take over and remove both of their clothing quickly and efficiently.

She needed to feel his skin against hers, to enjoy it before either of them had time to rethink this madness. His lips teased her earlobe, kissing a hot path down the side of her neck. He flexed himself against her, clever hands peeling the fabric of her bra down so he could take one hard nipple into his mouth. Goose flesh spread down both of her arms and she braced herself against the rough surface of the tree trunk in an effort to remain standing; the pleasure was so intense.

He growled against her skin and she threaded her fingers through his hair, holding him in place as he worshipped her breasts. She hadn't realised how much she needed this. The tension of the past few days seemed to ebb away with every long, languorous lick of his perfect tongue. His hands followed the curve of her waist down to her skirt, pulling the fabric upwards. She felt cool air on her upper thighs as she impatiently reached back and pulled the zipper downwards so that the material could be pulled up around her waist.

He paused for a moment, something dark and unreadable in his narrowed gaze, before he took her hips in both hands and held her tight against the evidence of his arousal. His fingers hooked into the lace of her panties and pulled them to one side, giving him direct access to the hot centre of her. With each small circling of his fingertip, she tightened and moaned, grinding up against him. When he slowly slid one finger inside her, she thought she might expire completely. Her mind short-circuited, and for a brief moment of madness she wondered if her body might have forgotten what it was supposed to do.

But Liro clearly wasn't worried. He growled words of encouragement, asking if she needed more. She was vaguely aware of herself nodding, begging, until he added a second finger. Almost immediately, she felt as if she was seconds from shattering, emotionally and physically. She had resigned herself never to feel like this again, and now here she was, running headfirst back into the fire. Her barely contained moans only seemed to spur Liro on.

She bit down on her fist, fearing they might be heard if she completely lost control. He pulled her hand away from her mouth, his eyes dark pools of desire as he worked his magic.

'Come for me,' he urged under his breath. 'Let me hear you.'

She did as she was told, breaking apart in sensuous abandon and crying out without any regard for decency. She felt as though her body was unravelling with every slick movement of him inside her, the pleasure so intense she thought she might cry with relief. She was vaguely aware that he had begun stroking himself during their interlude and, before she even had the clarity to try to return the pleasure he'd given her, he growled low in his throat, his own release taking him over. It felt painfully intimate, watching him lose control so quickly, as though they had gone straight back in time to their trysts as young lovers.

For a split second, she worried that this was the moment the bubble would burst. But then Liro took one long look at her and cursed under his breath, leaning down to take her lips again roughly. Minerva melted into his kiss, her mind refusing to come back to earth after the intensity of her orgasm. She had forgotten what it was like to completely surrender herself to passion like this. To lose herself in it.

But, as he took a step back to clean away the evidence of his own pleasure, she felt the first cold breeze of reality threatening to creep back in. The silence spread between them as he helped her to put her dress to rights, his strong hands smoothing the ivory material back down over her hips. It was a strange thing, silence. Minerva imagined it like a wave of icy rain, snuffing out any embers of desire that might have remained. It created a distance between them, far more uncomfortable and insidious than words could ever achieve.

Minerva ducked her face away from his gaze, feeling so vulnerable and over-exposed she could hardly bear it. She could feel his eyes on her the whole time and glanced up to see a deep frown marring his brow. He reached out, brushing some leaves from her hair, and her chest tightened at the tenderness of such a simple gesture. But still, he didn't speak.

She cleared her throat softly, forcing herself to stand tall and look at the man who stood silent and looming a short space away. 'The auction starts soon… I have to go back.'

'I'll walk you.'

'We both know it's best if you don't. I can't risk anyone finding us together…digging into your identity.' She shook her head, holding herself at a distance. 'This has to stop now, this *thing* between us. It needs to stop.'

'That would certainly be the most sensible course of action,' he drawled.

'It's the only course of action. Unless you fancy blowing up your fancy new life and inciting a royal scandal.'

'If anything, the revelation would cause Magnabest stocks to rise. I choose to live a life of privacy because it suits me. It brings me peace…' He looked down at her. 'You should try it out some time. I think life at sea would suit you…the sun kissing your skin while you recline on the deck…sea salt springing your hair into the wild curls they always make you tame down… Would you let me take you on an adventure, Min?'

'Perhaps. If things were different…' she whispered. He'd moved closer again and she swayed into him for a brief moment. His warm breath fanned the

**YOU** pick your books –
**WE** pay for everything.
You get up to FOUR new books and a Mystery Gift...
absolutely FREE!
**Total retail value: Over $20!**

Dear Reader,

Your opinions are important to us. So if you'll participate in our fast and free "One Minute" Survey, YOU can pick up to four wonderful books that WE pay for when you try the Harlequin Reader Service!

As a leading publisher of women's fiction, we'd love to hear from you. That's why we promise to reward you for completing our survey.

IMPORTANT: Please complete the survey and return it. We'll send your Free Books and a Free Mystery Gift right away. And we pay for shipping and handling too! *We pay for EVERYTHING!*

Try **Harlequin® Desire** and get 2 books featuring the worlds of the American elite with juicy plot twists, delicious sensuality and intriguing scandal.

Try **Harlequin Presents® Larger-Print** and get 2 books featuring the glamorous lives of royals and billionaires in a world of exotic locations, where passion knows no bounds.

**Or** TRY BOTH!

Thank you again for participating in our "One Minute" Survey. It really takes just a minute (or less) to complete the survey... and your free books and gift will be well worth it!

If you continue with your subscription, you can look forward to curated monthly shipments of brand-new books from your selected series, always at a discount off the cover price! Plus you can cancel any time. So don't miss out, return your One Minute Survey today to get your Free books.

*Pam Powers*

# "One Minute" Survey

## GET YOUR FREE BOOKS AND A FREE GIFT!

✓ Complete this Survey  ✓ Return this survey

**1** Do you try to find time to read every day?
☐ YES  ☐ NO

**2** Do you prefer stories with happy endings?
☐ YES  ☐ NO

**3** Do you enjoy having books delivered to your home?
☐ YES  ☐ NO

**4** Do you share your favorite books with friends?
☐ YES  ☐ NO

## YES! I have completed the above "One Minute" Survey. Please send me my Free Books and a Free Mystery Gift (worth over $20 retail). I understand that I am under no obligation to buy anything, as explained on the back of this card.

☐ **Harlequin Desire®**
225/326 CTI GRTQ

☐ **Harlequin® Presents Larger-Print**
176/376 CTI GRTQ

☐ **BOTH**
225/326 & 176/376 CTI G294

FIRST NAME _____ LAST NAME _____

ADDRESS _____

APT.# _____ CITY _____

STATE/PROV. _____ ZIP/POSTAL CODE _____

EMAIL ☐ Please check this box if you would like to receive newsletters and promotional emails from Harlequin Enterprises ULC and its affiliates. You can unsubscribe anytime.

HD/HP-1123-OM_123ST

delicate skin below her neck. It was such a wonderful fantasy of relaxation; she could almost smell the sea breeze on the air. She swallowed hard against the knot of emotion that had formed in her throat, meeting his gaze. 'But we both know things are not different. I have to go… It's my—'

'Your duty, of course.' He nodded, one hand rubbing the back of his head in a movement that seemed so tense and at odds with the passion of moments before. 'I suppose this was the one area of things that we never had a problem with.'

Minerva bit the inside of her lip, feeling suddenly cold. For a brief window of time, his strong, muscular body had felt so warm against her, so right. For a moment she had seen the old Liro, the one she had longed for all those years ago. But now, with this cool distance between them, she knew that he was right—they had always had sexual chemistry. Even when she'd known she was about to be forced to marry him, she had wanted to cling onto the passion between them like a sticking plaster.

With one final touch of her hand against his cheek, she turned and walked away. It took every ounce of self-control she had not to break into a run. She held her arms tightly by her sides, a deep shiver coursing through her, even though the early summer night was warm and fragrant. She closed her eyes, refusing to give in to the sudden wave of sadness that had turned her legs leaden and cold.

She would not cry.

She'd done enough crying over Prince Oliveiro of Cisneros to last her a lifetime; she wouldn't do the same for his new alter ego, no matter how much more beautiful and confident he had become. She had spent years believing that she had got over the boy who had broken her heart, only to realise that the break was only held together with tape. Now it felt as if that tape had split, leaving her feeling just as raw and vulnerable as she had on the day she'd realised he'd abandoned her.

She'd chosen to kiss him and open all of these feelings back up again. She'd let him touch her, let him give her pleasure… The idea that this place, *their place,* was now the scene for yet another goodbye between them was an unbearably cruel twist of fate. But at least this time she knew that was what it was. At least, this time, she had been the one to walk away.

Liro had no idea how long he remained beside the lake, trying to calm down the riotous beating of his heart. When he finally emerged onto the open palace grounds, the long driveway was filled with cars. Elegant guests in tuxedos and evening gowns ambled around the gardens, bathed in the glow of the lamps. He walked alongside them, not caring that he looked dishevelled and unkempt in his sand-coloured chinos. He hadn't planned to attend the auction, not when Minerva had made it so clear that she wanted him gone. So why then did he find himself wandering through the glass orangery? The soothing sounds of string music enveloped him, the scent of exotic plants filling his lungs. A waiter passed by him with a tray full of drinks. Liro grabbed two.

It was the correct order of things, he reminded himself as the first glass of whatever kind of alcohol it was burned down his throat. Minerva was about to become queen, for goodness' sake. While he… Well, he had never fitted into royal life, even when he had been a prince. As if confirming his thoughts, an older woman passed by, glaring down at his informal attire, and Liro let out a harsh laugh.

This world placed so much emphasis on how one looked, how closely one kept to the narrow paths assigned to every member of 'polite' society at birth. There was nothing polite about how people stared at him as he stood in their midst, daring to have his sleeves rolled up and tattoos on display. He knew that he looked every inch the sailor he had been for the past decade. Minerva knew that too. He had always despised the confines of this world, chafed against it. So why, then, was he so resistant to leaving?

His father had blamed his youngest son's yearning for freedom on selfishness. They had never spoken again after the day he'd demanded Liro propose. Liro had believed himself selfish too, for a long time. He'd believed any number of terrible things about himself, a natural result of being raised in such a hostile environment. He knew now that he wasn't terrible, but that didn't mean he was good.

A good man would have felt remorse for what had just happened with Minerva at the lake. A good man would have left the first time she'd told him to. He knew that he wasn't good enough for her—that had never been up for debate. But Minerva had been so wound up and desperately in need of care. He knew how to care for her. He knew what she needed.

He took a slower sip from the second glass, staring down at the ice cubes floating in the amber liquid. He had hoped to give them both some form of closure, a thought he had believed he could achieve. But, as he had watched her walls return in the wake of the orgasm he'd wrung from her body, the world had crashed back in upon her shoulders... and he had never felt further from closure with Minerva Argimon-Talil.

His mind balked at the idea of leaving without finishing what he'd started, without proving to her that their memories were not exaggerated. Maybe then he would feel free of whatever hold over him their connection had. He had come to Arqaleta to make a business deal, and that had not changed. But he refused to leave things the way they had been left fourteen years ago. It was his fault that she was being forced to choose from a ridiculous selection of thoroughly unsuitable potential husbands.

He could never have her himself; he knew that. He knew that he would never be the man that she chose. He knew that their lives were too different and utterly incompatible. But he was just selfish enough not to care right now. Not after he'd been moments away from burying himself deep inside the woman he'd chased from his dreams for years. Not when he'd seen how badly she still wanted him too.

A plan slowly formed in his mind, a perfect way for them both to have closure and for him to give her what she needed. He would have to ensure that he played his cards just right…and maybe this trip wouldn't have been completely in vain.

# CHAPTER SIX

THE CHARITY AUCTION was little more than a glorified gala dinner, and an excuse for the kingdom's wealthiest and most famous individuals to dress up and be seen. The palace's large greenhouse had been arranged into an enchanted forest, with invitees taking part in an Arqaletan colour theme for their outfit choices. So far, Minerva had spotted at least seven gowns covered in bows and arrows, as well as a handful of unfortunate banana-yellow tuxedos that seemed to be aiming for the colours of their national flag.

Everyone watched one another in the way that was typical for these events, where the aim was simply to be on display. There was the added bonus of being able to flaunt one's wealth in the form of bids, but for most part it was the kind of pageantry through which Minerva had to grit her teeth.

This was the first time she had been in charge of selecting the various organisations that would benefit, a fact that made the opening speeches and endless greetings slightly more tolerable. She had insisted that the founders and beneficiaries of each charity be present and offered the chance to speak if they so wished. Everything had been planned in the weeks beforehand; perhaps that was why her complete lack of focus hadn't impeded the plans too much.

Her gown for the evening had been designed and hand-made here in the capital by one of their most famous up-and-coming couturiers. It was an off-the-shoulder confection of white silk and delicate blue beading that accentuated her waist and fell to the floor in extravagant waves. It was a gown made for movement, and it had taken most of her control not to twirl herself out on the dance floor as she had as a young girl. Her mother had beamed at her upon first glance, with a genuine look of surprise that there had been no complaints from her only daughter about the matching sapphire tiara and heavy necklace she was displaying as part of tonight's ensemble.

Truthfully, Minerva had hardly been aware of much of the past hour since returning to the palace. She'd nodded and smiled as her team had readied her, and discussed the details of the auction portion of the event, but mentally she'd replayed every salacious moment of the events by the lake.

Even her mother had commented on her distraction, and Minerva had tried to make an effort to pull her focus back to the present. She tried to remind herself how inappropriate today had been. How nothing good could ever come of it, of them together. But tell that to her rioting libido.

She had gone on a few dates in college, experimenting like most young people did. But, as a young royal, all her relationships had to remain secret, or else risk being on the front page of every tabloid. Secrecy, while temporarily exciting, had always ended up being a real mood-killer at some point for the people she had been attracted to. Pretty soon, she had stopped even trying to date, allowing her archery career to take up most of her time, and had returned to her duties in Arqaleta once she had graduated. No one had got under her skin the way he had.

Perhaps no one ever would.

She entered the grand ballroom, spied him standing on the opposite side of the room and the knot in her stomach only tightened further. She hesitated, knowing that ignoring him would be immature, but she truly didn't think she could be face to face with him in that moment without losing her composure completely.

He'd said he sought closure for them both but she hadn't had any need for it until he'd reappeared in her life like a ticking time-bomb. She had not thought of him; she had trained herself not even to think of him most of the time.

But as she crossed the room towards him, his eyes tracking her every movement with his usual leonine intensity, she felt something much more than discomfort building within her. She was excited. Seeing him here, meeting his eyes and knowing what they had almost done mere hours before… The dark thrill of it seemed to sizzle along her veins, filling her with the confidence to meet his gaze without any guile.

His eyes narrowed upon her, his nostrils flaring with awareness, and for a moment it was only them in the bustling crowd of well-dressed guests. Another moment in time called to her from the recesses of her mind, another evening of dancing and revelry in this very greenhouse that had first begun their short-lived affair. An affair that had ended with her in tears and him banished. She closed her eyes against the onslaught, opening them to find him moving towards her in the crowd, a look of intent upon his face.

Her anxiety piqued, panic climbing her throat as she tried not to see the parallels between that night and this one. She couldn't speak to him, not tonight. She was here to secure her future, not rehash a past she'd long buried and grown past. Did he believe her too proper to cause a public scene? Maybe she should show him exactly how much she had changed.

It turned out she didn't have that chance, because she was pulled away by the event team before Liro had even reached the middle of the dance floor. Her presence was needed on stage to prepare for her hosting duties while the announcements were made and the guests were seated in rows.

A string quartet began the evening's entertainment, and Minerva tried to enjoy the glowing music. But her eyes were constantly drawn to the man seated at the very edge of the front row, his attention firmly placed upon her.

The first items of the night were a selection of beautiful traditional Arqaletan paintings and statues. The bidding was healthy, but not a war by any means, and the items were sold off with relative ease. Minerva took turns with the chief auctioneer in announcing each lot, and even began to have genuine fun in slamming the gavel down, earning laughter each time.

Liro did not find any of this amusing, it seemed. His gaze remained serious and pensive as he surveyed the stage from his perch, his wide shoulders making him appear so much larger than the others.

When the final lot of the evening had been announced and sold off in quick succession, Minerva breathed a sigh of relief, hoping to make a quick exit to regroup before her inevitable showdown. She smiled and made to leave the stage, only to be stopped by the curator, who gestured to where her mother had stood from her seat, microphone in hand.

'There is one final surprise for this evening, a very special lot offered up personally by my daughter in honour of my birthday.'

Bea, seated in the front row alongside her elderly parents, met Minerva's gaze in confusion. Minerva shrugged, communicating with her eyes: *I have absolutely no idea.*

Queen Uberta continued, 'My daughter is excited, ladies and gentlemen, for tonight she will be auctioning off none other than a date with herself. For the highest bidder, you can have dinner and startling conversation with the Crown Princess Minerva of Arqaleta.'

Movement and chatter began immediately, the auctioneer smirking as he took control of the proceedings and guided Minerva to take a seat under a spotlight in the centre of the stage. Training and experience meant that her smile was relaxed and her posture didn't give away the extent of her unease. She looked down to find Liro's seat empty, her eyes darting to each side of the room in search of him, but he was nowhere to be found.

The bidding began and was instantly off to a quick start as John, Jean-Claude and Prince Lorenz calmly raised their paddles one after another without any sign of surprise that Minerva was the lot in question. Had they somehow known about this particular portion of the auction in advance? Was that why Liro had disappeared? The thought that he had chosen *now* to abandon her to her matchmaking duty, as she'd ordered him to, was suddenly utterly despairing.

Minerva looked to her mother, silently begging her to announce that this was a practical joke. Sadly, it was not, and soon the bidding began to intensify, Jean-Claude scowling as he bowed out, leaving only her other two suitors to compete. She wondered what on earth kind of dinner date she would be forced to endure.

Likely it would be Lorenz, with his much deeper pockets, but something about the prince still didn't feel quite right. None of them did, though she didn't wish to break her mother's heart by saying such a thing. She had made a promise to select one of these men as her future husband by the end of the week and she did not break her promises—most especially, not to her mother.

Prince Lorenz called out another bid, doubling his previous one and leaving the other men to stare at him in stern silence. A moment passed, then another, and Minerva gulped, resigning herself to the idea that she would be back to discussing performance techniques in college sports again some time very soon.

The auctioneer smiled, gavel already raised to pronounce the sale, when a smooth voice rang out across the chatter of the excited crowd.

'I'd like to double that.'

Minerva looked to find Liro had reappeared in the same spot he'd vacated, looking utterly bored and unruffled, as though he'd been there all along.

The auctioneer stuttered, calling out the final figure with a question. Liro nodded, his expression utterly neutral as he stared in the direction of the prince. Lorenz scowled, shock and disbelief warring on his finely chiselled features for a long moment before he sat down, placing his small white number firmly in his lap.

'Sold, to the handsome ginger fellow at the front,' crooned the auctioneer.

Minerva was furious.

As if it wasn't bad enough that Liro had paid an exorbitant amount of money for one dinner with her, but he'd done it in front of an audience, advertising his position as one of her suitors. Then, after he'd signed the contract for their date, he'd simply disappeared. No discussion, no opportunity for her to tell him exactly how inappropriate and inconvenient his little stunt was. Not to mention no chance for her to ask him why he'd done it, when they had already agreed that he needed to leave Arqaleta before his identity was discovered. He'd simply left without a word.

When a note appeared with her morning post, requesting her attendance on his yacht later that evening, she felt her irritation peak. No, he would not send for her at his convenience. Her schedule was empty that afternoon, in preparation for the grand ball tomorrow evening, and again that niggling voice of suspicion within her wondered if her mother had deliberately organised it that way.

Ignoring that thought, she showered and changed out of the chic linen suit she'd worn to that morning's poetry and arts event which she'd attended with a very forlorn Jean-Claude. The Frenchman had been predictably attentive and apologetic about having been unable to win her in the auction. As had the others, when they'd approached her for dances after Liro had disappeared. Prince Lorenz in particular had been bordering upon rage as he'd not so subtly questioned her about the red-haired shipping magnate who seemed so intent upon monopolising her time.

Blood pounded in her ears as she stalked across the lawns in the direction of the port, the wind lapping her unbound hair and the plain black smock-dress she'd grabbed in her hurry. If he expected a princess for dinner, he would be sorely disappointed. She fully intended to tell Liro exactly where he could shove his bought date for the evening. That was, until she arrived down at the dock, to find the man himself standing on the bow of his mega-yacht, dressed in a pair of ripped jeans and nothing else.

She had wondered what Liro might look like as a sailor. Judging by the way he easily hoisted a thick rope between his hand and elbow, twining it round and round, calling across to his crew and giving orders, she'd imagined he'd looked pretty much like this—like a handsome, ginger-bearded pirate, getting ready to set sail across the seas in search of adventure.

She had thought that her travels with the archery team were thrilling—she had travelled all across the world, hadn't she? She had been given more freedom than her mother had ever dreamed of—a fact that the Queen reminded her of often enough.

But…she had never seen someone look quite as free as Liro did in that moment, the slightly cloudy sky shielding his fair skin from the harsh sun while the wind ruffled his thick red hair back from his forehead. The natural colour of his hair was even more mesmerising out here on the water. The richness of the bronze-red captivated her and made her fingers itch to run through it.

She gave herself a mental shake, clearing her throat, but the noise was drowned out by the sounds of the docks. Liro still had his back turned to her and was deeply engrossed in whatever he was doing with the heavy rope. He was working hard enough that sweat coated his brow and glistened on his bare shoulders as he heaved and pulled the rope around a large steel pole. The tattoo she had spied running up his forearm was in full view now, a winding design in black ink that formed an intricate sleeve across his right arm, shoulder and upper pectoral muscle. Minerva licked her suddenly dry lips, trying to ignore the mental image her treacherous mind produced in which she actually got to feel those muscles in greater detail…

Of course, he chose that exact moment to turn

around, his green-grey eyes meeting hers with pure
brazen confidence as he smiled broadly.

'You're a bit early for dinner.' His deep voice carried easily.

'I'm not here to eat,' she shouted back, crossing
her arms over her chest as he moved down the ladder
from the upper deck, coming to a stop at the open
gangway directly across from her. He leaned against
the railing, eyeing her up with the kind of slow precision that made her skin prickle.

'You look pretty hungry to me, *princesa*.' His lips
quirked. 'Have you looked your fill already?'

'I wasn't *looking*, I was…staring.'

'Staring at me,' he clarified helpfully.

'You're practically naked up there, for goodness'
sake!' she blurted. 'If I were to do the same, I'm sure
I'd get some odd looks too.'

He laughed, closing his eyes for a moment as he
gripped the railing hard.

Minerva growled under her breath. 'Liro, I came
here to…'

He raised one hand to stop her. 'Hold on, I'm just
trying to get a proper visual in order to make an informed rebuttal.'

'That is grossly inappropriate.' She fought not to
laugh as he appeared to concentrate even harder, his
eyes remaining firmly closed for a few more seconds.

'You're right. If you were up here topless, winding
rope, it would be catastrophic for this whole crew.'

'Catastrophic?'

'I'd have to have them all fired, of course. Anyone who'd laid eyes on you would be severely punished.'

'Including you?' she asked, enjoying their back and forth far too much.

'Oh, I wouldn't need to look, of course,' he said smoothly, the smile leaving his lips. 'I close my eyes and you're right there. Always.'

As she stood frozen in place, he raked his gaze over her slowly, from the top of her head all the way down to the strappy flat sandals she wore on feet. He met her eyes once more, showing her a brief glimpse of burning heat that took her breath away. It was the kind of look that she should have immediately turned tail and run from, if she'd had any sense. She was already too unsettled by this interaction, by *him*, to make the imperious speech she'd planned.

'You had no right, bidding on me last night. Why did you do it?'

'I don't like to lose,' he said, without a hint of remorse.

'You said yourself that you were never in the running.' she replied, fighting the urge to growl at the superior look on his impossibly handsome face. 'You say that as though you believe that this stunt has resulted in you winning.'

'You're here, aren't you?'

Minerva fought the urge to launch herself towards the ship to throttle him. 'I am not a commodity for you to bid upon or trade, or whatever it is that you are used to doing in your world.'

They were interrupted momentarily by the arrival of one of the yacht's staff, who needed Liro's signature upon something.

'If you have quite finished your speech, Your Highness, now that you're here, we might as well begin.' He turned to walk away towards the interior of the yacht.

'I have not finished.'

He paused but did not turn round, tension rippling through the ridiculously defined muscles of his gigantic shoulders. 'You wanted to discuss the past—this is the only way I will do that. I paid an exorbitant amount of money to have dinner with the Crown Princess, so get on the yacht.'

She hesitated, watching as he walked away from her and disappeared down a stairwell built into the polished wood. The question lay in the shape of the gangplank that separated them—five feet of wood and rope that separated her from the adventure he offered.

She remembered the wistful way he'd recounted his love of life at sea the night before. How he'd described it as healing, quieting something in him. This particular port wasn't quiet by any means, but the lulling sounds of the harbour had an oddly peaceful quality. For a moment she closed her eyes and simply listened to gulls cawing in the distance realising that, the longer she remained frozen in place, the further she was from getting actual closure on their past. Decision made, she boarded the giant yacht.

# CHAPTER SEVEN

STAFF AWAITED HER to take her bag and offer refreshments while she waited for Liro to return from wherever he was freshening up. She hadn't taken any security with her and noticed that Liro didn't seem to have any here either. She was shown to the entertainment deck, where a large open-air terrace took up most of the space, overlooking the lower-deck pool and hot tub.

She wondered how many wild parties this vessel had seen, how many women he'd entertained in his entertainment deck. He was a handsome man, not to mention a self-made owner of his own shipping empire. He probably had a woman waiting for him in every major port in the world. She stabbed her toothpick into a cherry and almost didn't hear Liro slide into the seat across from her.

His hair was wet from the shower and he had changed into a black T-shirt and jeans combo that hugged his thick muscles while still managing to look effortlessly stylish. She forced herself not to stare down at how the denim framed his strong thighs; she didn't need to boost his massive ego any more than she already had.

'This counts as your first course,' she said quickly, gesturing to the bowl of pretzels that had been placed on the table between them.

'Learning how to negotiate… I approve.'

His maddening smile irked her, even as she fought not to let her own lips curve. She wished that she didn't find him so entertaining, but it had always been this way. His dry humour was the perfect match for her, and he had always succeeded in pulling a laugh from her when most had failed.

But that was in the past. And if last night had showed her anything it was that their past would always be far too much to overcome. There were far too many things left unsaid, too much time had passed…and time was something she simply no longer had. Any other person at thirty-three would have had the luxury of time to consider what they truly wanted, where they wished to live and what career they wanted. But Minerva had simply been spinning her wheels for the past decade, never looking too far ahead. She had always known that one day the bell would ring and she would be obligated to fulfil the next step of her duty: a marriage of convenience, an alliance to strengthen her position, before she became queen.

There was only one person to blame for the fact that this cold reality now felt heavier than ever and he sat across from her at this very moment, looking as if he hadn't a care in the world as he stared out at the sea.

'Having me here on your yacht…is it supposed to have a specific effect?' she asked, idly twirling her glass. 'Am I supposed to see this lavish vessel that you've purchased for yourself and be jealous? Or did you hope I would be too distracted by you to remember that you had promised to tell me the truth?'

He was silent for a moment, his eyes scanning her face in a way that made him seem almost dangerous. He *was* dangerous…to her, anyway…to her plans, to her peace of mind. This man was a walking threat to everything she had fought so hard to contain within herself.

'This vessel is my home, Your Highness. I can give you the grand tour, if you like, once we're at sea.'

As he spoke, she became vaguely aware that the soft bobbing beneath her feet had turned into a rapid thrum. One look beyond the porthole behind her showed the harbour slowly slipping away from focus. She stood up, clenching her fists by her sides and looking down at him with full incrimination.

'Take me back to port!'

'I will, once we have completed our meal.'

'When I said I'd board your ridiculous yacht, I did not agree to leave the country.'

'You agreed to a five-course meal with me—the location is at my discretion.'

'You…you absolute *cheat*. Do you think that every tiny detail can just be manipulated and taken advantage of?'

'I do not cheat, Minerva. I pay attention to the details, in contracts and in people. How do you think that I went from deckhand to owner in less than a decade?' He met her gaze, taking the cocktail stick from her drink and popping the lush cherry into his mouth with a flourish.

Minerva walked to the railing and watched the edge of the palace grounds fade into the distance. She had no idea where he was taking her, no idea what he had planned. This date was turning into a living nightmare for a woman who lived her life on schedules and detailed itineraries. She had come here to take control and had wound up quite literally being swept away at Liro's will. She looked back to where he was watching her, his gaze completely unreadable, as usual.

Perhaps he was planning for some kind of poetic revenge. Perhaps Liro had hidden his cruel streak well and planned to steal her away, like the pirate she had accused him of being.

She shouldn't have felt a small thrill at that thought…and it had absolutely nothing to do with her capitulating and sitting back down on her seat.

Absolutely nothing at all.

* * *

Minerva remained mostly silent throughout their journey. It gave Liro more time to look at her, to think through exactly how he was going to talk about their past—something that he now knew he was going to have to do. As they disembarked onto a whitewashed marina and he guided her towards the street above, he had no need to slow down his pace, considering she almost matched him in height. She matched him in so many ways.

Minerva stood with her hands on her hips, eyeing up a small food truck surrounded by wooden picnic tables in the small seaside village where they'd docked. 'You sailed me across the sea to a mystery location…for food truck paella?'

'The *best* food truck paella you will ever taste.'

He waited a breath, fully intending to haul her back to the yacht and return her home if she ever actually said the words. But so far she had made a lot of eyes and grumbled but had not demanded to return. If anything, he felt she was relaxing into not being the one in control for once. As if she was almost enjoying their back-and-forth, just as she had when they'd been young.

Back then she had been the one who'd needed to be in charge, and he had simply gone along with it, happy only to be near her. So many things had changed, but the sudden smile that transformed her face was so youthful and reminiscent of that younger her that he remained frozen in place for a moment, almost forgetting that he was the one in charge of this date, until she nudged him.

'This is your second course and, yes, I *am* keeping track.' She looked around, her eyes landing on a large tourist sign proclaiming this quaint port town to be 'the Gates to the Cisnerosi Capital of Lodeta', which was a short drive away.

If she was surprised that he had brought her to his old home country, she didn't show it much. The only thing that had almost got a reaction out of her was when he'd presented her with a worn baseball cap and plain dark sunglasses.

'I've brought you here because, considering the history between Cisneros and Arqaleta, it's the last place anyone would think to find you. I wanted to give you something you haven't had a lot of: privacy.'

She looked around at the crowds of people passing them by and he could feel the tension rolling off her. He knew she had travelled to the Olympics, but always with a heavy guard. She had never been allowed to sleep in the team hotels or go out for spontaneous drinks in a crappy bar.

She'd lived her life on a leash.

He'd lived that life too and he'd despised every moment.

'Have you not been back?' she asked, looking around at the people eating at tables and looking out at the sea.

'I've been in the bay while overlooking my development plans here, but I never got off the yacht. I don't care if people recognise me. I don't need their forgiveness or adoration for all the work that I've done in fixing what my father ruined.'

His father had run their kingdom's economy into the ground through corruption, so it had been no surprise when people had mounted a coup. Liro hadn't known until it was too late, until the announcement of Minerva's and his betrothal was almost forced upon him by his father. And he'd rather Minerva suffer a broken heart from abandonment than have her name sullied by his father's sins and be bound in matrimony to Liro for ever. His father had died before he'd been brought to justice but his oldest brother, the crown prince, had spent some time in prison for the part he'd played. Liro hadn't spoken to either of his brothers since he'd left. Something a part of him regretted, despite their fraught childhood.

'I wish that I still had roots somewhere. Before my mother's death, things were different. He loved her and she calmed his worse impulses somewhat. I spent all of my childhood here, I grew up in this kingdom. But sometimes it feels like they erased my entire existence overnight.'

'When was the last time you actually set foot on Cisnerosi land?'

'I came back for the first time after being at sea for five years. I realised that I looked different and people didn't recognise me. And I liked it. So, I didn't tell them who I was, and I walked among them as a stranger in blissful solitude. And then, when the time came to set up the company, and as my success grew, I just kept burying my old self over and over until he no longer existed to me either. None of my family did.'

'Family is more than just blood. You can be close-knit without sharing an ounce of DNA, just as you can be hurt most by the people who gave you life in the beginning. I learned that with my dad—you can't choose who your parents are.' She exhaled slowly, folding and refolding the napkin in her hands. 'But you can choose how much of yourself you give them. The hardest thing I ever did was let go of my hope that one day I would have a relationship with him after what he did. Trust is a hard thing to rebuild once it's been broken by someone you love.'

Her words sat heavily in the air between them and Liro couldn't help but understand their meaning deeply.

'To our fathers.' Liro raised his glass.

After they'd finished eating, Liro took her to the funfair that had taken up residence in the town square for the summer. They walked through the fair and Minerva tried not to be nervous as people walked close by, jostling her shoulders. It was strange, walking with complete anonymity this way.

Liro insisted that they try out the games set on stalls dotted throughout the fair, hooking ducks upon a stick in order to win tiny soft toys. He won quite a lot of them on his first try, and kindly donated the toys to a group of children that had been standing watching nearby.

'That was kind.' She watched the children scamper away, taking their laughter with them.

'Your turn now.' He gestured to the next stall of carnival games.

'Darts?' Minerva raised one brow.

'It's not a bow and arrow, but I believe the practice is the same. Try to hit the pointy stick into the red dot.'

'I am familiar with the concept of the game. Thank you.'

'How about we make it a little more interesting, then?' He raised one brow, mischief in his eyes. 'You get one question for every target you hit.'

Minerva eyed up the three boards; they were hardly a far distance away. 'You may as well just give me the answers I want to know, really.'

'Perhaps—but my date, my rules.'

'Get ready to lose, then.'

She stepped up to the metal stall's edge, grabbing three darts. They were much smaller than her arrows, but weighed much the same. She stared at the oversized target, black-and-red rings with scores in each circle. A small smile graced her lips as she instinctively took her archer's stance and sized up the distance.

'Not taking it too seriously, I see,' Liro murmured from her side.

She ignored him, eyes focused on her target, shoulders dropping, arm relaxing as she extended and readied. With one long movement she let her dart fly directly towards the target in a perfect smooth arc.

Only to find it hit directly to the left of where she had aimed for. She cursed aloud, cupping a hand over her mouth when she realised what she'd said.

'It's okay, you'll get the hang of it with a little practice.' Liro laughed.

She ignored his taunts; she'd had years of training through the distraction of crowds and commentary. This was a funfair darts stall, not an Olympic stadium… You could take the athlete out of the competition, but not the other way around. She turned back to the target, once again taking her stance, readying her dart and letting it fly with perfect precision. And once again at the very last moment it flew to the left.

'Impossible.' She turned to the young lady behind the stall. 'This game is rigged.'

'Excuse me?' A man appeared from behind the stall, placing one hand on the younger girl's shoulder. 'Are you accusing us of practising dishonestly?'

Minerva opened her mouth to begin reciting exactly how she knew that this entire game was rigged for customer failure, only to have Liro grab her elbow and lean across her, placing a handful of bills on the counter.

'Of course she's not,' he said calmly, smiling at the young girl. 'She's just a sore loser, that's all.'

'I am not—' Minerva made to protest once more, only to have Liro's arm pull her into his chest and deftly guide her away from the stall before she could speak another word.

They made it a few more stalls down before she swung round, pointing one finger directly in the centre of his chest. 'Oh my God, you knew that these stalls are all rigged, didn't you?'

'It's a funfair, princess, not a global tournament. They're just trying to make a profit.'

'Does everyone know that nobody follows the rules except for me?' she practically shouted. 'You had no intention of answering any of my questions, did you?'

'Rule number one—don't assume that everyone else is following the rules.' He held her wrist, stopping her from moving away from him. 'I planned on answering your questions no matter what. Once we get back to the yacht, you can have the answer to everything you can think of. But I didn't bring you here to rehash the past. I brought you here to show you why I left. I could never live this way when I was Prince Oliveiro. I could never do what I wanted.'

'So that's why you left? Because you wanted to

be able to go to funfairs without the paparazzi following you?'

'You know that's not why…'

'I don't know, Liro. All I do know was that your father was forcing you to marry me and so you left. I thought we were happy, that we were preparing to celebrate our engagement. And then you disappeared and I had no idea if you were alive or dead. So forgive me if eating some paella and walking through a funfair doesn't feel quite as momentous…'

She walked away from him and was glad when he didn't immediately follow, giving her some space to browse through a small bric-à-brac tent filled with beaded necklaces and bracelets. She had no money with her with which to buy anything; she rarely made any purchases of her own at all. If she needed something, it was purchased for her, and for some reason she had never found that fact utterly ridiculous until this very moment. She was a grown adult and she had never browsed a store without a private appointment and security team in tow.

She realised then what he was actually doing in bringing her here. He was proving his point about freedom. Perhaps she should be annoyed at him for being so heavy-handed in trying to show her that the world was so much larger than the way she lived, but instead she felt a warmth in her chest. He had been more honest with her today in bringing her here and risking her wrath than anyone else in her life. He was showing her something real, something outside of her perfectly manicured sphere.

It was a gift.

She turned around to find he had purchased an aquamarine beaded bracelet, and he held it out to her. When she struggled with the clasp, he stepped closer, clicking it into place and sliding his thumb across the delicate beads. She looked up, meeting his eyes, and for a brief moment she wished that they were just a regular man and woman out on an exciting date at the funfair.

What would that actually have been like? What would they have been like if they had met under different circumstances? Would they have been so attracted to one another? Or had their love affair only happened because it had felt like a small rebellion of sorts?

And if she took him up on his offer of closure, if she went to his bed again, wouldn't that just be her doing the exact same thing all over again? She pulled away, walking slowly through the crowd, only to find his hand encircling her softly. This time, she didn't pull away. She relaxed into his hold and allowed him to guide her along, exploring together.

# CHAPTER EIGHT

HE HAD ALWAYS passed this particular summer fair as a kid, but he had never been permitted to go, much to his tearful disappointment. His father had teased him relentlessly for being soft and he'd soon learned to hold his emotions in check. It was possibly the only skill his father had taught him, other than how to stretch the truth.

He pushed away the uncomfortable echoes of his past and focused on the woman he'd tasked himself with unravelling in the present. Minerva was seated upon the tallest white horse in the merry-go-round, waiting impatiently for the ride to begin.

'I thought for sure you would have chosen the boat, considering they are your whole life.' She laughed down at him, her eyes still hidden behind her sunglasses.

'What can I say? This hot-pink princess carriage called to me.' He grimaced as his knee became wedged between the tiny seats. Better to make jokes than reveal he'd chosen it simply because it had a perfect view of the white stallion she'd selected. 'I know this will sound strange but I don't actually care about boats.'

'Liro, you have literally lived and worked at sea for more than a decade.'

'The whole ship-hand thing just happened; I didn't seek it out because of some unbridled love of the sea. I made a single promise to myself when I left, that I would go along with my instincts. And that's what I did.'

'I'm glad you trusted your instincts and you proved to yourself what you are capable of. I think you would have been quite bored by all of the sitting and smiling and waving—it is *not* for the faint of heart. Plus, you are huge now—we'd have had to have all the carriages adjusted.' She laughed, but he didn't miss the slight change in her tone.

'I never would have been bored with you, Min.'

'No?' She raised a brow.

'No. Not with you.'

Silence fell between them, only broken by the sudden tinny music that filled the air as the carousel began to move. Minerva smiled as her white stallion moved slowly up and down, leaning back to stick her tongue out at him and tell him to smile. Liro didn't smile—he was too busy watching. Back at the palace, the crown princess had been proud and regal. Beautiful, yes, but purposeful in every word and movement. Minerva unbound and free was… utterly breath-taking.

Her words played on his mind as they twirled round and round; her clear belief that he had left royal life out of boredom or disdain was wrong. In fact, he had fled to protect her from his father's crimes. Despite Liro being innocent of them himself, Minerva's court would never have seen it that way.

Once the ride stopped, he helped her down from her steed and tried not to laugh as she patted the painted horse's nose and thanked him for his service. Nearby, a large Ferris wheel spun in a slow circle to the sound of classical Cisnerosi folk music. Liro paid extra to have one small passenger car allocated just for the two of them. It was still early evening and no queues had formed. Parents and children began to fill up the rides around them, the noise of chatter rising and making it harder to hear, so he leaned across the space between them, reaching for one of her hands.

'You can be both, you know,' he told her, feeling the need to ensure that she didn't misunderstand him. 'You can smile and wave as their princess while also remaining true to who you are—the athlete, the woman.'

'You don't have to placate me, Liro, I'm quite aware of the pageantry of my position.'

'You were born to be the queen. That's the position you were trained to fill. It's a role that you had no choice in, but still, you were made for it. But Minerva the archer needs to be challenged, to feel in control and to feel like she is facing a new target, at all times.'

Golden-brown eyes met his, the lights of the funfair blinking around them.

'You can be both the queen and the archer, Minerva. You can be anything that you put your mind to. If anyone in this world can change a kingdom hundreds of years old to suit them, it's you. Push the boundaries, don't accept the cage for what it is.'

'Are you talking about my role as queen or what I must do before I ascend to the throne?'

'All of it,' he said honestly. 'You can call it whatever you want—it is someone else telling you who you are and who you can be. You are accepting it because there is a law involved, but you won't know for sure until you push.'

'What about the rules you set—can I push those too?' she asked sweetly.

'I wish you would.' He breathed, not bothering to temper his reaction to her words or to the images his mind created instantly at just how he wished those rules would be broken. No kissing, no touching… He had thought of little else every minute with her by her side and it was sweet torture to see her tongue dart out and lick at her lower lip. She bit down on the wet flesh, shaking her head softly, as though trying to clear similar images from her own mind. Did his princess have filthy thoughts too?

'Why would you make a rule that you have no intention of abiding by?' She breathed, her cheeks definitely flushed a little darker than they had been a moment ago.

'If I planned to break my own rules, I'd have done it the moment I had you alone on my yacht. That's not what today was about.'

'Then what was this about?' She frowned.

He leaned back, staring out as the fairground became smaller and smaller below them. 'I told myself that I just wanted to give you some time away from the pressure of the palace, away from your duty. Some time for us to get closure before I leave.'

'I want closure too,' she said softly. 'But I don't think I'm going to get that from a funfair.'

'What would you do, then?' he asked. 'What do you need?'

Her lips touched his, tentatively at first, as though she was feeling her way onto uneven ground. He wasn't even sure when she had moved into the seat next to him but, once she had grown certain of him, she inched closer until her thigh practically splayed across his. She angled her face, her hand touching his beard and holding him in place, and he let her. He submitted to her kiss, knowing that was what she needed from him in that moment. She needed to trust in her own ability to break the rules he had set for them both, and thank god…because he had been one step away from kissing her senseless from the moment she had appeared at his yacht, eyeing up his naked chest.

When the wind picked up and their car began to rock side to side, he used the momentum to his advantage, lifting her to straddle his thighs fully, her centre pressed full against the evidence of his arousal. Far from being scandalised, his fearless princess simply ground her hips against him and carried on plundering his mouth, using him for her pleasure in the best way possible.

If this was all he could give to her, he'd do his duty over and over again. He wouldn't think of the consequences, of whatever came after, when she returned to reality and remembered why this was wrong for them both. It was only when loud laughter intruded upon their little bubble that they realised the Ferris wheel had moved around a couple more places and their bucket was now fully visible to the riders above them. A horrified elderly couple tutted loudly, while above them a group of young men wolf-whistled.

Minerva scrambled off his lap, making to move back to her seat, but Liro wound his arm around her waist to hold her close. She looked up at him, her eyes still a little kiss-drunk, and it took all his restraint not to haul her back onto him, audience be damned. Her hair had begun to escape her cap, curls rioting around her face as she threw her head back and laughed. And, without even thinking, he laughed with her. The wheel brought them back down to the ground but Liro handed the attendant another wad of cash to send them around again, this time buying up all the buckets around them too.

'Seems like a lot of effort to get me up here all alone,' she remarked, a slight hint of uncertainty in her gaze. 'Did you plan to finish what we almost started?'

'You'd like that?' he murmured against her neck, memorising the feeling of having her all to himself again. No interruptions, no audience to play for.

She sighed into his touch. 'It would be wild, reckless—so very out of character for a good girl like me.'

He growled low in his throat. 'You don't kiss like a good girl, Min.'

'How do I kiss?' She bit down on his ear. 'Well, I hope?'

'You are perfect.'

Their eyes met for a split second and he saw the glazed-over desire there, the heady wildness of a woman in over her head. But he couldn't help feeling that this was too much, too fast. That, if she had a moment to think it through, she'd realise that this wasn't actually what she wanted. He'd already pushed her onto his ship and taken her out of her comfort zone. If he followed through now with what she very obviously wanted to do, sure, it would be amazing…but for how long? Once reality returned, and they quite literally dropped back down to earth, would she hate him all over again?

He had entered into this ridiculous game of match-making for closure, for a way to draw the line under their past. But somewhere during the past few days he had begun to think less and less of the freedom he adored so much. His thoughts had become consumed with her. After more than a decade of control, he was fast becoming addicted to Minerva once more.

She sensed the change in him, pulling back on his lap. 'What's wrong?'

'Nothing is wrong. The sunset is beginning.' He gestured behind them, to where the sky had blurred from blue to pink and purple around the setting sun. He turned her in his lap, holding her steady…not quite able to not touch her.

'Why do you do that?' she asked softly, leaning back against his chest with a sigh. 'The minute I stop fighting you, you get cold feet and go off into your own world. It always maddened me when we were younger.'

Was that what he was doing? He frowned, holding onto her hand as she sighed and laid her head down upon his shoulder to watch the sky transform. He had always told himself he simply preferred his own company, that he just didn't need friendships or connection. He'd learned from a young age that his quietness wasn't accepted, that the things he enjoyed would be mocked.

But he wasn't a child any more—he was a grown man. The realisation that his retreat might not have been entirely to protect Minerva was uncomfortable and something he could not accept. He had loved her…he had wanted to be with her…but he had known she deserved more than him. Deserved more than her reign as queen to be tarnished and criticised because of his tainted name.

As the glowing sunset erupted and the outside world blurred into a sea of colour, Liro couldn't shake the feeling that he carried more baggage from his childhood than he was willing to accept. Could such things really shape a person's actions for their entire lives? Surely not? He hadn't been beaten or neglected. He'd grown up a prince, for goodness' sake.

'I rather feel like I should have paid for this date, not the other way round.'

Minerva stared out, calm and still as she watched the crowds below them. This was a glimpse of the carefree princess he'd fallen for all those years ago before he'd ruined everything—this wild, free creature.

And she wanted him, she had made that much abundantly clear. She had to know that he would not deny her whatever she asked of him. He would not deny that getting her into his bed had been on his mind from the moment he'd walked back into her palace and laid eyes on her. But did that mean he should just take what he wanted, knowing that, afterwards, he would have to walk away and leave her to marry another?

He was so lost in his thoughts he hardly noticed the ride had stopped until he felt a hand gently pull at his elbow. They disembarked and wandered out into the rapidly increasing evening crowd of the fair.

A small stand was placed near the exit gate, selling tiny bags of sugar-coated nuts. He'd loved the smell of them as a kid. He watched as Minerva wandered closer, raising one brow in his direction.

'Looks like it's time for our final course.'

He didn't speak, paying for one bag and watching as she half-heartedly nibbled on the sugar coating. They strolled along the path to the marina in silence, her barely eaten bag of sweet almonds soon discarded in a waste bin once they had boarded the yacht.

'You didn't like them?' Liro asked.

Minerva hesitated, her gaze filled with a mixture of anticipation and a little uncertainty, an uncertainty that he knew he had put there. 'They weren't what I wanted.'

'You can't always get what you want.' He pushed her back against the door, turning the lock deftly in one slick movement before bracing one hand above her head.

'Are you about to burst into song?' She breathed, making a light attempt at laughter that quickly died once she felt the evidence of his erection against her.

'Oh, Liro…please don't stop again this time. I don't think I can bear it.'

'I won't be stopping, princess. If this is what you need… I won't stop until you're satisfied.'

'This…you…are what I need, Liro. Just you.'

He closed his eyes against the sensation her words unravelled in his chest, clenching his jaw against the foolish words he felt rise up his throat. Words that had no place there. His time with Minerva was destined to come to an end and once it did he needed to let her go, even if it tore him apart. Without thinking, Liro closed the gap between them and began to give Minerva exactly what she needed.

'I'd be lying if I said I didn't take you out today aiming for this to happen. From the moment I saw you again, this is all I've thought about—your sounds, your taste.'

Minerva watched as Liro dropped slowly to his knees before her. 'You have haunted me, Min, possessed me.'

His hands framed her naked centre, spreading her wide in a way that could have made her feel vulnerable and exposed. But instead she felt rather like a sculpture on display in a museum, scandalously adored and coveted. But he had no need to want her from afar, not now when they had so little time. She reached down and cupped the back of his head, pressing herself against his kiss without a hint of embarrassment or shame.

Those emotions could wait for the morning, along with everything else.

It had been so long since anyone had touched her. And this was so much more than the touching and kissing they'd already succumbed to; this was more and yet somehow it wasn't enough.

*Will it ever be enough?* that small voice whispered in the back of her mind.

Minerva tried not to let her body shake as she accepted the onslaught of Liro's attention. His mouth moved against her with devastating precision. She looked down to where his strong hands played along the skin of her stomach and thighs, snaking round to grip her behind and pull her closer to him.

He had never been this confident, this domineering, before. It seemed as if, without words, he knew exactly what she needed and where she needed it. But she had never been so eager to be dominated before either. Memories of their time together seemed to fuse with the present. They had been young back then, with no experience, nothing to compare to. They had simply been lost in their excitement and passion for one another's bodies. But now, with so many years between them, she felt doubts cloud her mind even as she tried to enjoy the ripples of pleasure working through her body.

'Stop thinking, Minerva,' he commanded, pulling

back to look up at her. 'Stop thinking about whatever has you so tense and give in to me. Give in…and I swear I won't stop until you are completely satisfied.'

'It's not that easy.' She gasped, shocked when she felt his grip tightening on her upper thigh, holding her in place.

'You need me to switch off your thoughts another way?' He looked up at her, his mouth glistening with the evidence of her arousal. It was so torrid, so utterly wrong, and yet when he stood up and kissed her she revelled in that explicit action. It seemed to break through a barrier in her mind and she leaned into him, kissing him back with the wild abandon that she'd been holding in check. She'd been holding herself together for fear that, if she let loose, she would unravel completely, irreparably, never to be put back together again like some broken thing. Hadn't she been broken for so long already? Maybe this was exactly what she needed. Maybe, as he said, they needed closure in order to move past the place where they'd become stuck.

A snap decision made, she leaned into him, her fingernails digging into his shoulders as she raised her thigh to bracket his thickly muscled hip. She moaned and ground the evidence of his arousal against her, separated only by a thin layer of her lace underwear. He was so hard, so large and, gods help her, she wanted nothing more than to climb him like a tree. She wanted to stop being angry and take what she was owed.

She would take this one night…one night without thinking like a princess. One night to feel just like a woman—his woman.

It was as if he sensed her change of thoughts, how her resolve had solidified her decision in the way her body had changed towards him.

'There you are.' He growled, tracing kisses down along her neck.

'This night.' She gasped. 'This one night is ours.'

The loose sundress that she wore was bunched around her hips and she could feel the cool breeze of the night air on her legs. He lifted her as though she weighed nearly nothing and carried her over to a canopied day-bed. It provided slightly more privacy than the open top deck, but not enough that she didn't feel the thrill of possibly being caught.

'No one will disturb us.' He growled, setting her down slowly as though she were made of glass. He looked uncertain as he stared down at her, and for one prolonged, awful moment she thought he had reconsidered this madness they had both willingly agreed upon. If he'd been thinking, he quickly came to a decision, smiling as he pulled her panties away from her body in one smooth movement. The sound of lace tearing was unbearably erotic, as was the glimmer in his eyes as he took a moment to obviously savour the bare flesh he had uncovered.

His eyes were dark and thoroughly locked upon Minerva as he moved over her, bracketing her in with strong arms and tracing one long kiss up her centre. This time, he would not stop until she was thoroughly satisfied—wasn't that what he had said? She didn't look away; she watched him as he pleasured her and sighed loudly as her release began to build. He added two fingers, curling them just where she needed them, and the pleasure built even further.

Liro's low, rasping compliments moved around her, echoing under their cocoon along with her increasingly harsh breaths. She was coming apart, losing herself. When he felt her begin to tighten, he commanded her to *just let go* and, to her surprise, she did. She let go of it all, shattering over and over again until her lungs ached from crying out and her mind was completely blank. When she became aware of herself once more, she only wanted one thing: him.

'Make love to me, Liro. Now,' she said, stretching her arms above her head and offering herself to him fully to do with as he pleased. She didn't care if he was gentle or rough, only that it was him, and they were together.

# CHAPTER NINE

LIRO RAISED HIMSELF up over Minerva's thoroughly pleasured body, his biceps bulging with the effort of not plunging into her immediately. He was too worked up after seeing her fall apart like that for him, too close to losing control, and he hadn't even thought to bring a condom. But then she'd asked him to make love to her, so very sweetly...and he'd been a lost cause.

'*Si, princesa,*' he murmured against her lips as he fought not to notch his hard length against her. 'We need to get protection, then you can use me as much as you need.'

She shuddered against him but then stilled, her golden eyes spearing him in place. 'I'm not using you, Liro,' she whispered, breathing hard as she punctuated her words with soft kisses along his chest and jaw. Her hands traced his pecs and his tattoos, coming to rest right above his heart. He closed his eyes against the vulnerability he saw there, the softness...

He'd been prepared for the frantic wildness of their initial joining, knowing that, so long as it was just sex, he could give her what she needed. He could be the man who made her orgasm over and over and still walk away at the end. But this... Having her look at him like this was almost more than he could bear. So he took the coward's way out and gathered her into his arms, carrying her into the darkness of his bedroom. He didn't turn on the lights, knowing exactly where to find the small square box of protection in his nightstand. He'd never brought anyone here, not even for a date. This had been purchased with Minerva in mind.

'I can't see you.' She laughed huskily, reaching for him.

'Use your other senses,' he commanded, moving behind her and sneaking a quick kiss on the back of her shoulder before grabbing her wrists and holding her in place.

'How can you see a thing?' She asked, out of breath from their play. Liro could just about make out the curve of her lips as he laid her down on her side, sliding himself behind her and entering her in one hard thrust. She inhaled a sharp breath that turned into a groan as he filled her fully.

'Tell me what you need, Min,' he murmured against her ear, using one hand to hold her thighs apart but firmly in place, stopping her from rocking against him.

'I need you…to move.' She gasped, craning her neck to seek out his kiss.

'Like this?' he asked softly, moving the barest few inches before stopping again. She moaned in protest so he moved again, the scantest couple of inches, before stopping.

'Liro, please,' she half-laughed, half-begged.

'You want more?' he said silkily, withdrawing completely and lying back on the bed. 'Don't ask me, don't beg. Take it from me, *princesa*. Take what you need.'

'I… I can't see you.' Her voice was a husky murmur as she turned over, hands outstretched.

'You'll find me.' He watched, jaw clenched, as her hands found his skin and she guided herself into his lap. He didn't know why he was playing games, only that he needed this. He needed to know that it wasn't just him going out of his mind with need here in the darkness of the night. He wanted her to be fully in control—maybe then the ache in his chest would ease. Maybe then he could stop counting down the hours until this night would be over and he returned her to where she belonged. To the royal life in which she had been born to flourish, the kind of world to where he could never follow.

He wasn't the right man for her in the daylight but here, under the cover of darkness, he knew that he could give her everything she had always been afraid to demand. He could show her the power she had over him, the power she had always wielded with effortless grace. If only she knew…

He waited patiently as she guided herself over him, resisting the urge to enter her as hard and fast as he had before. Teeth gritted, he hissed as she slid tentatively down onto his length with a sigh. He couldn't see her face but only imagine the satisfied smile he might find there.

Suddenly he regretted the decision to move them into the dark—he wanted to watch her as she took him. Reaching over to the bedside table, he flicked on a lamp to its lowest setting, bathing the bedroom in soft amber light. Sure enough, the sight that met his eyes was more beautiful than he could ever have imagined.

Minerva's eyes were heavy with pleasure as she found her own rhythm, her hands braced on his abdomen and her breasts… *Dios*, her breasts…

This was a queen seated atop her throne, conquering him with every slow circle of her toned hips. She used her thighs to grip him tighter, urging him to move faster and deeper and, after the slightest moment of resistance, he complied, smiling as she took exactly what she needed over and over again until he was the one falling apart under her control. She leaned down to kiss him as her own release sent her body into spasms and she finally went limp against his chest.

Liro felt as if he'd been hit by lightning, unable to

do anything for a long time other than run his fingers along her dark curls and hold in the words that threatened to spill from his lips. When he felt Minerva's breathing deepen, he arranged her onto the pillows alongside him and waited for the silence of the wide, open sea to soothe him to sleep as it always did.

But there was no soothing the ravaged beast that he had awakened within himself tonight. He'd been a fool to think that having Minerva in his bed one more time would be enough. He knew that he could not have her, but he had meant it when he'd said she shouldn't have to marry at all.

His mind moved over the various possibilities that they might both get what they wanted but came up short. It seemed that, no matter which path they chose, one of them was destined to lose something important. And he knew that, if he had to choose, he would take that loss himself.

Every time.

Minerva awoke in the circle of Liro's arms, her face pressed tight against the centre of his chest. His eyes were closed, his face peaceful, and she took a long time just simply to look at him. Never once had they fallen asleep all of the times they had been together as young lovers. Their meetings had always been rushed and secret, overshadowed by the worry of being caught. Last night Liro had come through on his promise not to stop until she was satisfied. They had made love twice more after that first time.

With no clock or watch to go by, she could only guess that they had slept for a few hours: the sky outside the portholes was still pitch-black, but with a tinge of violet to signify that dawn was not far off. Dawn meant that her day of freedom was officially over...and, with it, her time with Liro. She moved slowly out of the circle of his arms, sliding her bare feet down onto the plush sand-coloured carpet. Her body felt heavy, warm and satisfied in a way she didn't think it had ever felt, not even after her most gruelling Olympic training sessions.

She stared around properly at the lavishly decorated space for the first time, taking in the inner sanctum of the powerful shipping mogul he'd become. Despite the obvious wealth and quality of everything aboard his yacht, Liro's bedroom was quite warm and minimalist in its appearance. A tall shelf of books filled one wall, coupled with a comfortable-looking arm chair that faced out towards the tall windows. There were no family photos or mementos, but it felt lived in. Liro had said he'd chosen this vessel as his only home and she could feel that was what it was.

His bathroom was almost the same size as the main room, with a large double tub and a shower stall that took up the entire wall towards the end. A surprising ache formed in her chest as she spied his toothbrush sitting in a cup by the sink along with the mint-flavour paste. She stared at the mundane items that filled the open vanity cabinet, studying them, needing to know who he was. How he had lived for all these years when they had been apart.

She stepped into the shower stall, closed the door behind her and stared up at the confusing high-tech display. Her eyes unfocused as her mind continued to race. Had Liro brought other lovers here? Had they shared his bed and used this luxury shower the way she was doing now? Frowning, she tapped a few buttons, gasping when cold water instantly streamed down over her body. She frantically tapped the display again until it turned off, leaving her shivering but kind of thankful for the jolt away from her uncomfortable thoughts.

Everything about his world made her feel out of her depth: the fancy appliances, the lack of rules and routines. She knew nothing about this version of Liro, only that he wanted closure from their past just as she did. He said he had thought of her, sure, but had he missed her the way she'd longed for him? If he had cared half as much, surely he wouldn't have been able to leave? She leaned her head forward, seeking the cool, glossy wall tiles to calm her racing thoughts, only to see a shimmer of moonlight on waves.

This was not a wall at all, she realised with a start,

but a window. She gasped aloud, covering herself with two hands.

'It's one-way glass,' a voice murmured from behind her. Minerva instantly moved to cover her bare breasts and relaxed once she saw Liro sliding open the shower door and stepping inside. His red hair was ruffled from sleep, his face slightly flushed. He looked infinitely younger…almost like the young man she'd once known.

She might not be able to name what he meant to her but she knew it wasn't just freedom, a warm body to use or any of the things he had accused her of. It was more that he had always meant more to her than he was supposed to.

'I didn't know how to work it.' She gestured to the shower and stepped back as he moved around her, fiddling with the display. Hot water fell from the wide waterfall-style attachment above and the scent of lavender essential oils filled the air.

'You don't look as blissfully relaxed as I hoped you would after last night's efforts.' He frowned, one large hand cupping her cheek. 'Talk to me, Min.'

'I'm okay,' she said quickly, avoiding his eyes and how much they always saw. He moved closer, caging her in against the glass as the steam whirled around them.

'You're lying,' he said. 'Want to know how I know?'

'How?' she whispered.

'Because I'm not okay either,' he murmured. 'I

woke up alone in my bed…and I thought you'd gone back. And I wasn't okay, Min. I wasn't okay at all.'

He leaned in, every inch of his warm, wet skin pressing against hers. It wasn't a sexual embrace, it was comfort. She closed her eyes, feeling the emotions within her peak. How could a night feel so perfect and so terrible all at once? How could one person be everything you needed and everything you could never have?

She felt the final wall she'd built to keep him out fall and crumble. This day…all the emotions he'd made her feel, all the pleasure…had torn away all the defences she'd spent so long creating to keep herself safe. Now she was raw and fourteen years' worth of emotions had risen to the surface.

'Why did you have to leave?' she heard herself whisper. For a moment, she thought the noise of the water might have drowned out her needy words, but she felt his body tense, his head dropping down to her shoulder.

'I already told you—it was the best thing I could think to do. I didn't know what my father had done but, even so, marrying me would have ruined you.'

'I understand why you walked away from the betrothal. But why did you leave *me*?' she said, not bothering to hide the tremor in her voice. 'You never even thought to talk to me first. Never thought to say goodbye.'

Minerva watched him rub a hand along the back

of his neck, his jaw tight as he stood up straight under the hot spray. He looked tortured, his throat working as he tried to speak, then he gave up, shaking his head. 'I should have. I wish I had.'

'Did you know that I always hoped to see you?' she whispered. 'Every city I travelled to, I looked into the crowds and wondered if I would see you. I always hoped…'

'And if you'd found me?' he asked softly, his voice cocooning her in the steamy air.

She turned away. Of course she understood his meaning, even if it hurt. What *would* she have done? Would she have abandoned her duty and run away with him? Would they have lived out their days in the bowels of a shipping freighter? Or would he have stowed her away in some port city, returning every six months?

'I left the way I did because I didn't trust myself to say goodbye,' he said, his hands sliding down to sit heavy on her waist. 'You were just having a fling, determined to perform your duty by marrying me. But Min… I was in love with you.'

His words snapped like a whip in the silence, stealing the breath from her lungs as she let them sink in. She couldn't move, couldn't do anything but stare out at the thin line of the approaching sunrise beginning to peek out from the inky-black horizon. She closed her eyes, feeling his deep sigh against her back.

'Why didn't you…?' She bit down hard on her lip. 'You never said.'

'You remember how shy I was. I barely spoke for the first few summers. But I watched you from afar.' He laid a gentle kiss on the top of her head, turning them so that the water warmed their rapidly cooling skin.

'I think I fell in love with your confidence first—I was captivated by how determined and capable you were in everything you did. How kind you were to everyone, even the awkward, scowling prince who followed you around the palace grounds. I was always drowning in my own thoughts, my own insecurities, but when I was with you… I could breathe. So, yes, I fell in love with you long before my father revealed our betrothal. I thought that maybe your feelings for me would develop and we might make things work. But then that day…'

He didn't need to clarify what day he meant; she knew. Every failed relationship has one—the day that changed everything. The day that sealed their fate. She had seen misery in his eyes but had thought it was his own regret at being forced to marry her.

'I asked you why you wanted to marry me,' Liro continued. 'And, with your reply, I saw myself through your eyes. I saw how things would be, with you calmly taking me on as a husband of convenience while I pined for you. I was young and impulsive and angry—so angry. The idea of having you but never truly having you… In my mind, there was no other option but for me to leave.'

The light in the bathroom revealed more details hidden within the curling tattoo designs that she had inspected before. The dark ink covered his shoulders fully but in the middle of the swirls she spied a familiar shape: their lake. And on the banks stood the dark silhouette of a woman gazing up at the moon.

'If you think I walked away and never thought of you, you're wrong. I carried you with me, Minerva. Right here.'

She placed her hand over his heart, drawing in the warmth from his skin. From the words she'd never known she needed to hear so badly—that she'd been wanted, loved even, even if it was all in the past. He had loved her once, back then. He hadn't just used her for her crown or played a part that he'd been forced to by his father.

She closed her eyes, wondering how different things might have been if she'd not been such a coward and kept him at arm's length. In her mind's eye she remembered his face, younger and so earnest as he'd asked her why she was going ahead with the wedding. As he'd gone cold at her abrupt answer. She'd believed herself to be the only one with a broken heart that night… Of course he'd run from her— she'd driven him away.

Now, here in the present moment, the idea of admitting that she had been in love with him too seemed utterly absurd. Would he believe her? Or would he see it as a pathetic attempt for her to rid herself of some of the guilt crawling up her skin, making her shiver? She closed her eyes against the force of her own regret and the desperate longing that came with it. She couldn't look at him, not when she knew she was so close to losing control and admitting everything.

Her love for him then…and now.

Because she suddenly knew without a doubt that nothing could possibly hurt this much and not be love. And it was absolutely terrifying. Shivers covered her skin, breaking open that small, vulnerable part of her that she'd kept hidden away. The part that told her that every man who claimed to care for her would leave, that no one was truly reliable or trustworthy. It was a hard, cynical way to feel and she despised it. Had she been so affected by her parents' relationship that she'd used it as a blueprint for all others?

She had never even attempted to bond with someone new after Liro, had never gone beyond the odd casual date if she felt like some fun. A small part of her had welcomed the royal marriage requirement as a way to appease the constant questions about when she'd find the one. She knew that, for her, true love and happy marriage would not exist, so giving herself a week to select a stranger to marry hadn't been a big deal at all.

Now, the idea of returning to Arqaleta and choosing another man as her husband made her feel wild with the wrongness of it. But they had both known that was the way it must be; they had made their deal knowing that this was only a temporary reprieve from reality.

'You're breaking your own rules again, princess.'

His voice stirred her from her thoughts. She looked up at him and thought she saw a brief mirror of her own pain before he stepped closer and pressed his naked body flush with hers. 'This time is not for talking and thinking about the past. Not when this is all we have.'

He claimed her lips in a scorching kiss that chased away all the overwhelming emotions that threatened to swallow her whole. In their place, it was only him—only Liro. He kissed her for what felt like hours, his hands in her hair. He kissed her like the drowning man he'd described, as if he was drawing in every breath of her.

# CHAPTER TEN

LIRO AWOKE TO the to the glorious sight of Minerva, fully nude, arranging a modest breakfast upon the table near his bed. He didn't move immediately to speak or alert her that he had awoken; instead, he simply watched her, taking in the graceful focus she put into arranging toast upon one plate and heaping some eggs alongside it.

She had cooked for him… He had let the crew take the night off once they had returned to the ship the evening before. The captain and a small skeleton crew would stay on the opposite end of the ship, where the engine room was, to ensure that all remained well on the vessel, but the cleaning crew and hospitality staff were gone.

'I can feel you staring.' She turned to face him, her eyes sparkling with mischief. 'I wore a robe when I went into the kitchen. This is pretty much the only dish I can make, so…'

'Does this count as course number five?' he asked, 'Or am I breaking your rules again?'

'I think we broke more than one rule last night.' She smiled shyly, hiding her face behind her dark curls as she laid their food out on a tray and put it in the centre of his bed.

He reached over, unable to stop himself from cupping her face with his hand and claiming her lips in a soft kiss. The kiss deepened and his simple need to touch her and taste her became more, his hands pulling her closer.

'The food will go cold,' she chided, sliding out of his grasp with a happy sigh.

The ate in a companionable silence. She poured his coffee, he buttered her toast. But all along he felt an undercurrent of tension building in his gut. He glanced at the clock that showed that it was almost eight, and he knew that her first event of the day began in less than an hour. Once they had finished eating and clearing away their plates, Minerva flopped down onto the bed, looking at him with hooded eyes and wiggling her finger in a 'come hither' motion.

Liro inhaled a calming breath, knowing that his body would doubtless hate him for what he was about to ask, but…

'I would love nothing more than to spend the entire morning in bed with you—you must know that.' He watched as the playfulness left her eyes, replaced with a guarded expression. 'You have duties to return to.'

'I took the day off.' She bit her bottom lip. 'I called my team and organised for my mother to run the event solo this morning.'

Liro froze. 'Why would you do that?'

'I thought that you would be pleased.' She frowned, reaching down to pull the sheets over her bare breasts, guarding herself from him. 'I was taking your advice and doing what serves me. But now I feel kind of foolish that I didn't ask you first. You probably made plans to sail off somewhere today. I can call them back, get someone to come pick me up.'

He stopped her before she could begin grabbing her things, hating the look of uncertainty on her beautiful face. 'Minerva, trust me, I would love nothing more than to disregard the shadow of your duty hanging over both of us. I would love to keep you here on my ship—'

'Then keep me,' she interrupted, reaching out to pull him towards her. 'Let's ignore the real world for a while longer. Let's pretend it's just me and you for one more day.'

He closed his eyes as her lips traced the skin below his navel, moving down. Her hands moved around to his buttocks, gripping him, holding him just where she wanted him. He let her take control, tilting his head back as his mind continued to work against his body. Common sense told him to force the issue, to prevent her from neglecting her duties and blaming him for it in the future. But another more selfish part of him asked…what future? This was it. This was all that he would get of her, this small window of stolen time that he himself had pretty much forced her to give him.

He had told her the truth last night—that he had broken the betrothal because he'd been in love with her. He'd spoken about it as though those feelings were firmly in the past to protect his own pride. But he knew his feelings were still there, raw and burgeoning against the surface of his control.

She'd seemed shocked at the revelation, but she hadn't said she felt the same. They'd made love again twice and now she wanted to stay…but did she want to stay for him or what he made her feel? That selfish voice within told him to shut up, to live in this moment and not invite reality back into their bubble.

In the end it was Minerva's lips that took control of the situation, pushing away all rational thought as she gave one long, languorous lick down the length of his erection.

'Still thinking about my duty?' she asked, her voice a husky rasp as her eyes met his and her lips worked his length, taking all of him in, worshipping him.

He couldn't speak, couldn't think, as her brown eyes held him in thrall, making him feel a depth of emotion he had thought he would never feel again. His hands wove through her hair, holding her with gentle deference as she brought him to climax with a swiftness and intensity that he had never experienced.

Her sweet smile as she looked up spoke of pride and victory. She had conquered him truly. He knew then at that moment that he would do anything for this woman. He finally admitted to himself that he had come back here for her, that he had received that invitation and immediately set sail for this island as though he'd been shown the way to a treasure he'd thought he would never see again. She was his treasure—she had been from the moment he had first laid eyes on her. He hadn't known how important she was to him then…not until he'd lost her. But now, taking her into his arms and holding her close, he knew that he would never allow anything to hurt her ever again.

But what if the biggest danger to her perfect future as queen…was him?

Minerva knew that she was playing a foolish game, prolonging their time together this way. But, as she watched Liro dive off the bow of the yacht, then smiling from the crystal-clear water below, she couldn't quite muster the energy to feel regret.

She could feel a shift in the air since his mention of her duty earlier. Perhaps that was why she had been so insistent on bringing him to climax that way for the first time. The power and the erotic pleasure of it had astounded her; she had already been halfway to an orgasm of her own simply from having him fully under her control and feeling him come apart.

Of course, a more sensible woman would have awoken the morning after a passionate one-night stand with her ex and immediately left to return to reality. Especially when that reality involved a very imminent and public elevation to queen of an entire kingdom.

But, when she had opened her eyes in the early-morning light and felt Liro's arms around her, she'd felt free. The idea of getting dressed and walking off his ship, going back to reality, had set a riot of angry hornets flying around in her mind. Her fingers had shaken as she'd typed out the email to rearrange her schedule. Just one more day, she'd told herself. Then she'd feel ready to walk away.

Liro crooked his finger up at her, mischief in his eyes as he trod water, waiting. She stood poised on the outermost ledge, taking a moment to feel the breeze in her unbound hair.

'What are you waiting for?' He laughed, splashing cool sea water up against her legs. Strong hands slid around her calves as he moved up against the side of the ladder.

'I'm not waiting for anything, that's the point.' She smiled, sighing as he gently kneaded the tension from her body.

'I'm surprised there's any tension left after the

amount of times you've made me come in the past twenty-four hours.'

'You were always this way.' He dropped a kiss on her knee. 'Strung tighter than one of your bows.'

She let a noncommittal sound escape her lips, her thoughts feeling more and more clouded by the minute.

'Do you miss competing?' he asked, pulling himself up to sit alongside her.

'Sometimes,' she said, leaning against his cool skin. 'I loved seeing the world and meeting new people. But some of the other archers saw me as a hobbyist rather than a serious competitor. There were many unfair terms thrown my way—some of it from jealousy or dislike, but some were deserved. I can be overly confident, maybe even a bit tunnel-visioned, when I want to do well at something. I was always conscious that I had a very privileged upbringing with some of the world's best trainers. Even if I lost everything, I returned home to a palace, which wasn't the case for my competitors.'

'You deserved your success, Minerva.'

'I worked hard but, once my mother told me of her wish to step down, it wasn't a difficult decision to leave it all behind, you know?

'What about you?' She tried to appear casual. 'Do you ever miss royal life?'

'I miss the version of royal life that existed before my mother's death. Being in Cisneros brought back some old memories that I'd forgotten. But that life doesn't exist any more.'

Minerva nodded, wishing she had the courage to ask the question she really wanted to: *would you ever return to royal life...for me?*

She closed her eyes against that foolish thought, tilting her head up to the sun as though the burning heat might chase away all the shadows that had begun to encroach on her little oasis of freedom. But an oasis was all that this could ever be—a temporary illusion of peace and tranquillity—no matter how much she wished things were different.

'You have shadows in your eyes again, Minerva.' Liro tucked his fingers under her chin, turning her to face him. 'Is this whole shipwrecked fantasy doing nothing for you?'

She laughed, loving how easily he made her smile. Loving *him*. 'You might have the luxury of being a runaway pirate prince, Señor San Nicolau, but I have to go back eventually.'

Liro's firm grip tightened ever so slightly around her wrists. 'If I were a true pirate, I wouldn't return you. I'd keep you right here.'

'Would you hold me to ransom?' She laughed. 'Make me walk the plank?'

'I'd tie you to the mast and have my wicked way with you for a while.' He nuzzled her neck, nipping his teeth against the soft skin there. 'Yes... I think I'd find endless ways to enjoy my stolen booty.'

'An endless booty call. Is that what we're calling this now?' She laughed. 'I don't know… I think you'd tire of me eventually.'

'A good pirate knows when they've found a treasure so rare they could never part with it.' Liro's eyes met hers and Minerva stopped breathing for a moment, fearing she might burst into tears if she spoke.

She fought to find the right words, wanting to lay out every messy emotion within her heart for him to see. He cared about her, that much was undeniable. *But he can never be yours*, that tiny voice within reminded her softly. Even if his identity wouldn't be a scandalous risk to public opinion about her;…even if he didn't run his own shipping empire with the world at his feet…deep down, she knew he was still the boy who had longed for freedom from royal life.

The royal role that she adored and worked so hard to keep was part of a life he despised. To ask him to consider being with her, when he knew that she needed to marry immediately, would be selfish. He had already been used as a pawn by his father years ago; she would never do the same thing to him. Not when he had told her how happy and peaceful his new life made him. He already had everything he had ever wanted…

Liro cleared his throat, ducking his head from her view. 'Of course, I'm not an actual pirate. Let's make that very clear for any Arqaletan coast guards who might be within hearing distance.' He raised both hands up for theatrical effect before he dove back into the water.

'Thanks for making that clear.' She chuckled to herself, pushing away her morose thoughts as she slid down into the crystal-clear water. It was warm and she welcomed the silence as she let herself sink down under the waves.

Liro's arms were around her in an instant, their bodies twining around one another and their lips meeting as they floated back up to the surface together.

Minerva woke to the sound of beeping. It was coming from her phone by the side of the bed. Eyes half-closed, she grasped for the device, jabbing her fingers at the screen until the noise stopped.

She lay back down on her pillow with a sigh. The room was quiet but for the sound of Liro's soft breathing. She turned towards him, taking the opportunity just to look for a while. It was late in the morning, and Minerva could stall no longer. Tonight was the grand ball and with it her mother's announcement. It was time for her to return to Arqaleta and do what she'd set out to do.

Unease crept up her spine, making her turn from Liro's handsome face as she pondered what must come next. She'd lain awake for a while last night, after she and Liro had spent a full day doing nothing but eating, laughing and making love. She'd forced herself to think of the practicalities, to prepare herself for her return home and the decision she would have to make.

Of all the suitors she'd entertained, Jean-Claude struck her as the most suited to the role of king consort. He was a descendant of European aristocracy, was handsome, confident and had excellent public speaking skills. She would set a meeting with him this afternoon, formally propose marriage and it would be done. Another item ticked off her list.

'Good morning.' Liro's strong arm curved slowly around her waist, his lips tracing kisses along her bare shoulder as he pulled her back against his gloriously nude body.

'Good morning to you too,' she murmured, melting into his embrace. He was hard and she was weak and one last time of having him inside her seemed like the perfect way to say goodbye really.

She laughed as he moved up over her, covering her with his full weight and spreading her legs wide. But, just as he made to enter her, another sound filled the room, this time a more serious tone coming from the intercom upon the wall.

'Ignore it,' she pleaded as Liro apologetically stood up and walked over to press the button on the intercom. She understood that aboard a vessel there might be emergencies... Well, at least she understood that on a logical level. It would take quite a lot of fire and brimstone for her to be happy about not making love with Liro again.

She watched as he spoke in a low voice. She could tell something was wrong as his eyes instantly darkened, his brows knitting together. He thanked whomever was on the other end of the line for telling him, his tone serious enough to have her sitting up straight in the bed.

'Who was it?'

Liro's eyes met hers, his expression starker than she'd ever seen it. 'My publicity team. My identity has been discovered and made public.'

# CHAPTER ELEVEN

MINERVA'S HEARTBEAT THRUMMED in her ears as she opened her phone screen to see a newspaper article published one hour ago. It had been sent by Liro's PR team, accompanied by no less than twenty-three missed calls in the past forty minutes since she had put her phone on silent mode. The article was headed: *Mysterious Shipping Magnate is Long-Lost Banished Prince!*

'Oh, God...' she whispered. 'How did they find out?'

'Someone was bound to eventually.' Liro stared blankly at the photograph filling her screen with an image of his younger self. 'I never intended to hide my past for ever. But I didn't plan for it to happen like this, when your kingdom is at such a pivotal moment.'

Minerva thought of her mother, of her vow to do whatever it took to repair Minerva's standing in public favour. She had been so close to fixing everything, so close to being ready to make her mother proud. To making her people proud.

Having this reminder of the past splashed all over every newspaper on the day her mother planned to announce her abdication wasn't just inconvenient... it was a disaster.

She turned, looking around the bedroom floor for items of clothing that had been discarded the night before. The bed sheets lay in complete disarray, towels strewn on the floor after they'd finished making love in the hot tub after a lazy dinner.

Everywhere she looked, she was met with reminders of their time here together. Not that she needed them. The memory of Liro's love-making wasn't something she would ever forget. Nor did she want to. She didn't regret it. She had planned to tell him that, before she left his yacht, but now everything was in chaos and she had no idea what to say.

She picked up her dress, throwing it over her body. There was no time to search for her bra, not when at this very moment her mother was likely hunting her down.

'Min, calm down. You can't just rush back to the palace like this.'

She shook off his grip, moving to step around him to find the rest of her things. 'I need to go and help with the damage control.'

He blocked her path. 'By damage control, do you mean rushing to announce your engagement to one of your mother's more appropriate suitors?'

Minerva sucked in a breath, feeling her chest ache. 'That's what I should have been doing all week, instead of running away. It's my fault that this is happening. I should have gone back yesterday.'

'Who is going to be the lucky man?' he asked harshly. 'The prince?'

Minerva shrank under his cold demand. 'Actually, Jean-Claude makes the most sense.'

Liro's grey eyes darkened to obsidian. 'All of this pageantry has been to bolster you in public opinion, to make the public view you as a suitable queen. What will people think now, Minerva, seeing their perfect princess walking off *my* yacht?'

He walked over to the balcony doors, opening them up to reveal the sound of shouting and commotion. Sure enough, a small crowd had formed further down the marina, held back by a makeshift barricade of Liro's security guards.

'If you rush out of here dressed like this, there is not a single person with eyes who wouldn't know what we have been doing all night.' He moved closer, staring down at her with that same intensity. 'Are you so eager to run off and select your new fiancé so quickly after leaving my bed?'

'This is how it needs to be.' She shook her head, 'It's my duty to my mother to fix this as soon as possible but I can't calm the press with you here. An announcement of a royal engagement to Jean-Claude will distract them for a time.'

'No.' Liro growled, wrapping one arm around her waist and hauling her up against him. 'I don't want you near him. I wouldn't let you off of this ship if I could manage it.'

'You've done your deal; you've had your closure... There's nothing else keeping you here.' Her breath heaved with the effort not to sink into him, to run back into the physical pleasure she craved. But this was so much bigger than them now: this was fast on its way to becoming a royal scandal.

'Your public image was already in question. You need to control this news to avoid disaster, Minerva. You need *me* here to control it.'

'You've admitted you had no public image at all for the past decade, not even with Magnabest. What good could you do?'

'We have been through this once before. Surely you know the answer?'

'No.' She shook her head against his words, shaking off the painful mirroring of their past and present. She wouldn't entertain history repeating itself this way—she *couldn't.*

'You need another announcement, one that would overshadow this one.' Liro met her eyes, cold and unemotional. 'We will announce our engagement immediately.'

Liro would have been lying if he'd said that this wasn't what some deep, dark part of him had wanted from the moment he'd set his course to return to this kingdom. He wanted her with every fibre of his being and the thought of having her by his side…in his bed, in his arms for ever…made some hungry part of him want to grab at this opportunity with both hands and make sure that neither of them could ever turn back.

He wanted Minerva for himself…but not like this.

'It would only make everything worse.' She shook her head, staring at him with the exact horrified expression she'd worn the first time they'd had this conversation. This time, at least, he had been the one to propose.

'Make the announcement, Minerva,' he said roughly. 'Your team know how to spin it as a grand love affair. The public will be appeased. Your mother can go ahead with her plans to abdicate. Two scandals solved for the price of one.'

'It would be that easy for you?' she asked, tucking her arms tightly around herself. 'You would marry me, walk back into this world?'

He fought off the instinctive discomfort that her words evoked—the memories of his younger self, of always feeling unsuitable and unwanted. Was that how she would see him now? She had been so ready to choose another as her king consort, to send him away. Perhaps a better man would have obeyed. But he was not a better man. He might not be her ideal choice for a royal husband but he was more trustworthy than any of the other men she'd been prepared to choose between.

'I was never guilty of the crimes my father committed. So, it's the best solution,' he said, avoiding her eyes lest she see right through this poor show of bravado. 'You would only have to remain married to me for a short time, long enough to get settled as queen. After a year or so, we could divorce. It's not as if that has not happened—'

She winced and he realised, far too late, the gravity of his words. Minerva did not speak of her father often, or the public divorce that had shadowed her early teenage years. He closed his eyes, pressing thumb and forefinger against the bridge of his nose. 'I didn't mean to speak ill of your parents.'

'No, it's the truth. The public have already recovered from one broken royal marriage. Seeing as history is already repeating itself, we may as well lean into the charade, right?'

'Minerva.' He moved towards her, freezing as she raised her arms up to hold him off, warning him not to come closer, not to touch her. How was this happening? Less than an hour ago, they had been blissed out from a second night of pleasure and now she could barely look at him.

'I need to return to the palace, Liro.' Her brown eyes were cold and flat, as though every ember of happiness had been extinguished within her. The idea that facing marriage to him had affected her this deeply hurt now, more than it ever had the first time. Back then they had been young and naïve and his love had been a fragile thing.

Now, it was deep enough that this rejection hurt like a knife sliding between his ribs. Like an arrow, aimed at him with every furtive look of disapproval she threw his way as she finished dressing and putting her hair to rights in the bathroom mirror.

But at least now he would not be foolish enough to hope that a marriage between them could be anything more than a temporary solution. He would not be so naïve as to believe she would come to do something as ridiculous as love him. But she would not marry the Frenchman or any of the others. She would marry *him*.

He had walked away from Minerva once, leaving her alone to pick up the pieces, and he would not do that again. The next time he walked away from Arqaleta, it would be once she was seated firmly upon her throne and needed no one else to keep it.

He watched silently as she slipped her feet into her shoes one at a time, her voice a low monotone. 'I need to speak to my mother alone. Discuss our options.'

'Discuss me, you mean.' He remained still. 'Because, if marriage is on your agenda, I am the only eligible bachelor you will be selecting.'

Minerva closed her eyes. 'You are…impossible.'

'You can keep fighting me, but we're not so different in this regard. Once I make up my mind on what I want, I get it.'

She shook her head, fists balled tightly at her sides. 'You don't want this. You don't—'

'What will you tell her about where you've been?' He cut across her anger. 'How will you explain how you of all people didn't know my identity?'

'You were gone a long time. I'll tell her I wasn't sure.'

'You recognised me the moment you truly looked at me, Minerva. You knew me.'

He waited for her to respond, not knowing what he wanted her to say, only that they couldn't leave things like this. He couldn't be about to become engaged to the woman who had haunted his dreams for so long only to have her look at him as if he was the villain of her fairy-tale. As if she despised him. Or, worse, as if she was completely immune to him.

Another brief window of happiness before the world came crashing in… His mind mocked him as he watched Minerva get escorted by his security team to a waiting car, cameras flashing from the crowd of photographers up the street.

Their time on his yacht would now haunt him more than any of his other memories of her. He had walked away once before; he had forged a new path for himself knowing that he was giving her the freedom she deserved. He would not do that now. He would marry her if she still wished for it. He would enter a royal marriage of convenience. He would do it…even if it tore him apart.

But he would not submit to it without ensuring she had every other option available first. She was only in this situation because of the rules of the world she had been born into. And, as he had told her many times, he did not often like to play by the rules.

Decision made, he tapped his phone to call for an urgent meeting with his team at Magnabest. Likely they were all still celebrating their win and planning for the huge development project that lay ahead for them. They would not be pleased with what he was about to ask them to do. But, as he looked from his office windows in the direction of the palace, he knew this was what he needed to do.

Once back at the palace, Minerva threw herself into damage-control mode. Her mother was absolutely furious in a way that Minerva had not seen in a long time. Public scandal was always a difficult subject for her to navigate, and seeing her usually calm, controlled mama so stressed brought a heavy sense of shame upon her.

The news of Liro's identity had swept through the kingdom with surprising swiftness, along with paparazzi photographs taken of them at the fair in Cisneros. The entire public relations team was already working overtime to try to ensure they had some control over the story.

'Minerva, honestly, I thought that you had more sense than to be photographed in this way! When were these photographs taken?'

'Two days ago…when I said that I was taking the evening to rest. Liro took me to a fair.'

'You were…not resting.'

'No, Mother.' She waited for the inevitable ranting to begin about her deception and her lack of care about her duty. She deserved it; she knew that her behaviour had been inappropriate and reckless… But still, she waited and nothing came. In fact, when she looked up into her mother's face, the other woman was smiling.

'I think your amusement is possibly more disturbing than the scolding that I expected.'

'Darling, you are a thirty-three-year-old woman who is readying to take over an entire kingdom. I am not about to scold you.'

'You're not?' Minerva frowned. 'I thought for sure that you would be furious. You invited him here believing him to be a shipping magnate, a catch…and it has led to scandal because of my inability to face the truth.'

Her mother shook her head, her eyes drifting away towards her secretary for a split second. A look passed between the women, a widening of the eyes that drew Minerva's attention instantly. 'Neither of you are surprised…and you both admitted to putting extensive research into your matchmaking solutions.'

Her mother grimaced.

'Please tell me that you did not know who he was… That you didn't seek him out on purpose?'

'That depends, Minnie, my love…did it work?'

'You lied to me. You had me sneaking around, trying to stop you from finding out, and the whole time you knew what were you doing? Placing bets on how big of a scandal this would bring down upon us all?' Minerva choked out the words.

'I chose your happiness over the threat of scandal, my love. You told me to choose you a selection of the best possible partners. I could not do that in good faith without inviting back the man that I knew you had loved, the young man that I wrongly banished through my own anger at his father.'

'What happened before was not your fault. I told you that.'

'It was not within my power to stop you from having your heart broken before, but I would not be able to allow you to enter into a loveless marriage of my own doing…if I hadn't at least tried to give you back the one that you deserved.'

Minerva felt hot emotion threaten to choke her as she processed what her mother had done. Of course her mother had known… Maybe she simply hadn't wanted to see that herself.

The love that she deserved… She thought of Liro's

offer of marriage and felt her jaw tighten painfully. 'I'm pretty sure that all of your meddling has been for nothing. We are right back where we were fourteen years ago—staring down the barrel of a forced royal marriage of convenience.'

'I don't see how. It's as clear as day to everyone that man is head over heels in love with you.'

'Any love he may have would be stifled by having to remain here. He hated royal life in Cisneros. He would rather have disappeared than remain here and clear his name.'

'This isn't Cisneros. And you are not nineteen any more. He knows what he wants.'

'You don't know that.'

'Don't I?' Her mother stood up, 'I have it on good authority that half of parliament met with the heads of Magnabest today. There was only one item on the agenda.'

Minerva stared down at the royal memo her mother placed before her, sent over from their prime minister to inform Her Majesty that their investor had placed a freeze on its plans until the Crown Princess signed off on it…as Queen.

'He can't do that, can he?' Her fingers trembled as she read the short memo again, hardly believing the ramifications of one simple act. In the time since she'd left him, it appeared that Liro had been in a plethora of meetings with her mother's parliament. He'd purchased the land and he owned it outright now. Freezing his plans would lose him valuable time in developing it—there was no logical reason for him to wait. Emotion tightened her throat painfully so that, when she finally spoke, it was with a hoarse croak.

'He's holding our government to ransom to ensure my succession.'

Her mother nodded. 'Tell me that is not the action of a fool in love.'

Minerva swallowed the pain of that statement, realising that there was a very real possibility that her mother was right. Liro had told her he'd been in love with her before everything had torn them apart. But the fact remained that she would become queen. She would remain here in this palace for much of the year, serving her people and carrying out the plans she'd spent years forming to make their lives better. This was her life's work, her vocation. There would be little time for spontaneous trips or adventures; everything would be planned and ordered. That was everything that Liro had told her he despised.

'I thought this would make you happy.' Her mother frowned.

'It does make me happy. *He* makes me happy, even when he's not terrorising the entire Arqaletan parliament in my honour.' Minerva felt bittersweet tears threaten, wiping them away quickly with the pads of her fingers. 'But the fact remains, I can't expect him to walk away from the life he chose to come and stand by my side. I can't force him back into the royal world that he despises, all in the name of love. Eventually, he will resent me. And we both know where that leads.'

Her mother's eyes widened with understanding and Minerva felt ashamed. She knew it was irrational still to be so affected by her father's abandonment, but there it was. When she thought of marriage, she thought of her parents and the circus that had been their very public divorce. Going through that with a man she barely knew had been a risk she'd been willing to take, but not with a man she adored.

'Minnie…your father never resented royal life, he left because he fell in love. Yes, it was selfish, and I wish he had taken more care with you. But our marriage was arranged and we were so different. The only thing we ever agreed upon was how wonderful you are. It was a relief when he asked for a divorce, even despite the scandal.'

'I just don't know if I can bear it.'

'You don't have to be the only one in this. Go to him. Let him make that choice for himself. Figure it out together.'

Liro stood at his office window and watched the kingdom of Arqaleta disappear behind him. He hadn't intended to leave today but, with a large storm set to come in tonight, his crew needed to pay a visit to the mainland. Truthfully, after a long day of arguing in a boardroom alongside Magnabest's corporate team, he needed space.

Since his identity had become known, he had felt more of an outsider than ever. His CEO had even attempted to bow to him when they had first met in the hallway. He had known the man for years, but it seemed hiding one's true identity under a persona made people upset. A fact he supposed he understood, even if he knew he had his reasons.

Still, he had done his part in ensuring that Minerva's future was made up of choices rather than just duty. He had seen the faces of the men and women who ran the parliament and had seen how they'd known instantly that their plans had been felled. And he had never been more glad he had trusted his own instincts.

She was free now, safe in the knowledge that she did not have to appease anyone by marrying in order to secure her crown. It was hers without question.

Maybe that was why he had chosen to remain aboard when his staff had informed him of their need to return to the mainland for the afternoon. The grand ball was to take place in a matter of hours, and he would wait and watch while the Queen announced her imminent abdication to the world. Minerva would become Queen immediately, but in essence she already was at this very moment. He had watched as the Prime Minister had signed it into existence.

And with it he had felt something within him tighten. Some deep-seated knowledge or old pain that, once she knew she didn't have to marry him, she would be relieved. He knew that she had not been false in her emotions during their night together. He was confident in her physical attraction to him, and their chemistry together. But as for her heart... She had never mentioned love to him, not once. She had never alluded to the fact that their relationship was anything more than just sexual, passion and freedom.

When she became queen, she would have no need for his adventures and freedom. She would be required to have almost every moment of her day accounted for and planned. She had prepared for this moment for her entire life and, while he was brimming with excitement for her and full of confidence that she would do amazing things, a small, selfish part of him still rallied against what he had done. He had almost had everything he wanted, and he had quite literally signed it all away when he had made the deal on behalf of his shipping company, ensuring Minerva had a choice in her life.

He was so lost in his own thoughts that he hardly noticed when the movement and the noise of the waves slowed, almost as though had they had begun to stop. He looked out and sure enough there was something amiss. A loud siren blared from outside as he opened up a porthole and stuck his head out to investigate. What he saw shocked him to his core.

Four Coastguard ships had surrounded them, the grand Arqaletan coat of arms emblazoned on their sides. Sirens blared along with a voice commanding them to come to an immediate stop and prepare to accept boarding. Liro pressed his intercom directly to the captain's cabin.

'What is the meaning of this?' he demanded.

'They are ordering us to return to shore,' the captain shouted over the noise of sirens.

Furious, Liro bounded out onto the deck in the direction of the part of the vessel nearest to their unwelcome visitors. He'd had quite enough of the government of Arqaleta trying to have its say in his business. He had absolutely no patience for this happening now. Rain had begun to fall hard and fast but he ignored it, climbing the emergency ladder to get to the captain's board fast.

It was only once he was high up on the top level that he looked down and saw a sight that sent his blood running cold.

'Minerva.' He breathed.

She was standing out in the rain, her blue sundress billowing in the gusts of wind as a team tried and failed to aim a rope-bridge device towards his yacht. She shouted something he couldn't hear, putting her hands out to take the device herself even as the men shook their heads.

'Don't you dare,' he hissed under his breath, frozen in place as he watched her take stance and aim.

The rope bridge unfolded and she looked up, meeting his eyes with triumph.

'No, Minerva, stay there.' He launched himself down the ladder, determined to reach her before she began the dangerous journey across. It was a short distance, but still the slippery rope and plastic were treacherous and all it would take was one wrong foot...

Terror striking his heart, he bellowed again for her to remain on her side, but she had already begun to make her crossing.

Minerva could just barely hear Liro shouting over the noise of the wind, the waves and her own frantic heartbeat as she tried to be graceful in navigating her way across the rope bridge they'd secured between the two ships.

'Stay where you are, damn it!' Liro roared, his voice reaching her on a gust of wind. She looked up to see him climbing down from the top deck like a madman as a handful of his staff watched.

Minerva looked back towards the Coastguard ship to find it was much further away than she'd thought. She was pretty much halfway now. Her knees buckled as her hands slid across the wet ropes, holding on tight with all the strength she had. She gritted her teeth, looking down at her sandalled feet moving one step at a time, until a wooden ledge appeared under her feet and she realised she had finally reached the other side. She barely had a moment to stand up before strong arms grabbed her, pulling her head up against a warm, hard chest. She didn't need to look up to know who it was—she knew Liro San Nicolau's heartbeat better than she knew her own.

'I told you to stay.' He growled, his hands in her hair as he tilted her head up to face him. 'You could have fallen to your death! You should have waited for me.'

'I'm the one who sent the full Arqaletan Coast-guard to stop you from leaving me—the least I could do was let them stay dry.'

'You thought I was leaving you?'

'Well yes, considering arrived down at the dock to find your huge, hulking yacht disappearing into the horizon.'

'So you armed your own armada to stop me?' His eyes were wild. 'My crew needed supplies from the mainland before the storm hit—we were only planning to be gone for a couple of hours.'

'Oh.' Minerva grimaced. 'I suppose I overreacted slightly?'

Liro stared down at her for a long moment, then he laughed, deep, barrelling laughter that eventually made her laugh too. The wind whipped her hair across her face and Liro pulled it away, studying the long curls that swirled loose around her shoulders with a sudden thoughtfulness. For a moment, she wondered if he planned to kiss her, but then his hands dropped from her face and he took a step back. 'Tonight is a big night for you, for your mother... I know we argued, but I wouldn't have missed it.'

'She told me what you did today. What you're risking.' She watched as his eyes darkened and felt a sliver of fear in her chest. A hint of doubt that maybe she had been foolish to assume he'd done all this for her out of love.

'Why did you do it?' she asked. 'Why not just go ahead with marrying me?'

'I wanted to offer us both another way.'

'I told you that I would not force you down the aisle.'

'There is no version of this life in which I would ever need to be *forced* to marry you, Min. Not then, not ever. I walked away from you once in an effort to save you, and in doing so I wasted fourteen years that I could have spent with you in my bed, in my arms, in my heart... I am selfish enough to grab this opportunity to make you my bride...but I loved you too much to have it happen this way.'

'Loved...as in past tense?' she asked. 'Because I know you loved me once and I came here to ask you if you could give me another chance. If you could love me again, the way I love you now.'

'Love...as in, every place, every time. Always.'

She threw away all her plans to be romantic and poised in her own declaration, throwing her arms around his hulking shoulders and pulling him down halfway to meet her lips. She kissed him with all the love she felt, all the fear and all the joy. She kissed him until the wind almost pushed them both overboard and the captain called out across an intercom for them to get inside to safety.

'Mad woman,' Liro drawled under his breath as he gripped her behind through her wet gown. 'I don't know anyone else who could have made that shot with a rope bridge in a thundering storm. You're terrifying when you're furious, you know that?'

She gasped as he climbed over her, tearing away her wet dress as if it was tissue, grumbling about her catching a chill. It was laughable to think her body would have the chance to get cold with him nearby. He had them both naked in minutes, his hot skin evaporating any rain water that dared to remain upon her.

'Ask me to marry you again.' She breathed as his hands began to travel down her stomach to where she craved him. 'Ask me to be your wife, Liro.'

She waited for his answer, her breath coming faster as his fingers found the centre of her and dipped in, drawing slow circles upon her right where she burned for him. Her practical mind argued that they should be fully clothed and serious as they discussed something as pivotal to their future. But, then again, so little about their relationship had ever followed the rules.

'God knows I have wanted nothing more in this

life than to hear you beg me so prettily, *princesa*. But there is something that would make me happier.' He paused, a smile transforming his lips. 'I want to watch you become Queen in your own right, just as you have always dreamed of. When I propose to you…when I finally claim you in front of the world as my bride, my wife, my queen…it will be because that is what you want.'

'What if I want it right now?' she challenged.

'I'd obey, without a question, Your Highness.' He smirked, placing a kiss upon her breast with reverence. 'When are you going to realise it, Min? If you decided that you want to get married right here, right now, I would do it. I would wear the giant crown. I'd be paraded through the entire capital in the open carriage, no questions asked.'

She laughed, feeling joy burst through her fears as he kissed her again, deeper and softer than before. A kiss that was filled with promises.

'I like your plan better,' she whispered. 'It feels almost like a normal courtship.'

'I plan on sneaking you out for as many dates as I can manage, Your Highness.'

They had soaked the sofa through with their clothes, and the storm outside was only picking up with every moment, but in his arms she felt warm and secure. He leaned down, pressing his forehead against hers.

'I vow to you right here and now that, whatever

our life needs to look like on the outside, you will have it. Because you have me. As long as we both shall live.'

# EPILOGUE

QUEEN MINERVA OF ARQALETA was crowned in late November, after six months of already acting as Queen of the realm. Her mother, a monarch globally known for her stoic manner, sobbed throughout most of the ceremony and sought regular comfort from the handsome ginger-bearded man by her side. Once the rumours of the banished and formerly disgraced prince had surfaced, it seemed that the public had been more interested in their relationship than in his family's unhappy past—a fact that they had decided to use to their advantage, giving tactical teases about their passionate love affair while simultaneously insisting upon privacy.

Their numerous romantic getaways had dominated the headlines of most of the world's press, bringing an unprecedented amount of attention to their tiny kingdom during the transitional period after her mother's abdication. The fact that the new Queen was still as yet unmarried had not been an issue. In fact, her public approval ratings were now the highest of any new monarch in the kingdom's long history. It seemed that the people of Arqaleta had been hungry for change, and Minerva intended to give it to them. Her mother had not fully disappeared from palace life, of course, and still took part in monthly summits discussing the future of their beloved kingdom.

A weekend of festivities followed the coronation, with not one but two public holidays declared to celebrate the coronation.

'I didn't fidget with the crown once.' Minerva smiled at Liro as they finally returned to their private apartment in the palace, shutting the door on work for the day. Here, they were just Min and Liro, and that was the favourite rule they'd made up once they had formally moved in together last month. He was upon her in an instant, his hands deftly pulling the pins from her hair and massaging her scalp as he pressed his nose to her neck and inhaled deeply.

'I know these big events with all of the public adoration are a part of the job, but damn if it doesn't get any easier sharing you.' He growled, pulling her closer to claim her lips with his. They had not had a single private moment all day and Minerva groaned into the kiss, relaxing into his quiet strength. This was her favourite time of every day. Their passion for one another had not waned much in the wake of their tumultuous reunion—they'd already made love twice that morning before they'd had to begin to get ready for the ceremony. But that did not stop Liro from lifting her bodily into his strong arms and bounding through the apartment in the direction of their bedroom.

'I don't know if the carrying is approved in the handbook.' Minerva smirked, tracing the perfectly trimmed edge of Liro's beard with reverence. He smelled like sea air, adventure and home. Even now when they were living full-time at the palace he still managed to make every single day feel exciting and rich with possibility. Truly, every reigning monarch needed a brooding ginger pirate by her side.

He laid her down upon the bed, removing both her shoes and throwing them away without any care for propriety. Her stockings were removed next, and then the skirt of her gown rolled up around her hips.

'I can take off the dress.' She laughed as he growled with impatience, burrowing his head impatiently under the material.

'And ruin my fantasy?' he chided, disappearing fully beneath her gown.

'Wh-what is your fantasy?' she asked, shuddering as she felt his lips tracing a slow, determined path above her kneecap.

'My fantasy, Your Majesty...' he murmured, emphasising each word with another kiss, 'Is that one day, in the distant future, we see this coronation gown in the royal museum...and I get to lean down and remind my queen of the time that I brought her to the best orgasm of her life while she wore it.'

His words scandalised her in the best way and she opened more for him, watching as he laid claim to her body in the most primal way possible. Her intimate folds were spread wide and his eyes met hers, silently demanding that she watch him as he tasted her in slow, teasing strokes. His mouth conquered her slowly and completely, sending her into a haze of incoherent babbling within moments as she begged, 'Yes…' and, 'There…' and, 'Please, Liro, please…'

He knew just how to hold her right there, making her beg for just the right amount of time before granting her mercy. His name was wrung from her lips on a shocked cry as she fell apart, blissful waves crashing outwards through her body and leaving her boneless in a cloud of silk and tulle.

*Happy Coronation Day, Queen Minerva*, she thought with a giggle as she let her head drop back onto the bed.

Only then did he unzip her dress slowly and free her from the restrictive fabric. He had a strange look on his face as he undid each tiny button and hook on her complicated corset, his fingers stroking along her skin where it was marked from the pressure. Tears pricked her eyes as she realised he was always there to kiss her better in the aftermath of whatever her day had involved. He had become her own personal island kingdom in the sea of obligations and duty—her home.

Consumed with the need to reciprocate and show him just how treasured he was, she took advantage of his apparent distraction and flipped him onto his back, stranding him before he could protest.

'This was not part of my plan just yet...' He began to speak, stopping when she slowly angled herself to notch his impressive erection and rolled her hips in a tease. His eyes narrowed upon her, his breath leaving him on a low hiss as his head fell back onto the pillow in apparent surrender.

Minerva's victory was short-lived as their sensual haze was immediately interrupted by the sound of scrambling paws in the distance. Moments later, a small ball of honey-coloured fur bounded through the doorway in a chorus of high-pitched barks. Liro quickly covered them both with the coverlet just before the mischievous pup jumped up onto the bed to join them.

'Flecha, down!' Minerva made an attempt at a stern voice, trying not to laugh.

'I told you, now that you've let her sleep here once...' Liro chided, rubbing the ear of the excited pup while she made quick work of trying to chew Minerva's antique pearl earring from her ear.

'She missed us, didn't you, *mi amor*?' Minerva crooned, laughing as Flecha attacked Liro's foot under the covers.

An impromptu sailing break that she and Liro had taken along the northern coast of Cisneros the month before had ended with them finding a new-born pup abandoned on the beach. After taking the pup to a local shelter for medical attention, and confirming there was no owner missing their pet, Minerva had been surprisingly bereft at the idea of leaving her there.

Liro had been the one to suggest they adopt her and he had also suggested the winning name—Spanish for 'arrow'. Together they had worked their schedules so that one of them was always close to their newly renovated palace suite. But, for times when they were away, she had employed a royal dog-sitter just for the occasion. She watched as Liro beckoned the pup to come back to his side of the bed and tried not to laugh as he again tried to teach Flecha the 'sit' command.

'You know, *darling*, I am queen now...independently, as planned,' she mused aloud, wondering how to broach the next subject without seeming completely overbearing. Which she knew she kind of was, but hadn't he said he loved her taking control?

Liro paused for a split second in his dog wrangling. 'Yes, I was there.'

'It's just... I was thinking... Well, actually, it was my mother who made the observation earlier that, while the people have been quite accepting of our unconventional union for the moment...'

Liro sat back, a strange smile on his lips. 'Are you okay?'

'I'm fine. I'm better than fine! I'm so happy, I truly am… I just kind of thought you'd have gone caveman by now and challenged me on the "no ring before the crown" agreement.' She lost her nerve, standing up to pace the room. 'It's unbearably self-ish and ungrateful, because now I have the home and the crown, and even a puppy for goodness' sake, and I just—'

'*Minerva!*'

She snapped up her head, noticing the odd way that Liro was holding their squirming pup in place upon his lap. She looked closer and saw that a square pink box had been tied to Flecha's little pink collar.

'Oh, it's a… *Oh.*'

Liro tried not to burst into laughter as he realised he had succeeded in rendering the Queen of Arqaleta absolutely speechless. She took a step back, eyes wide above the perfectly manicured hands she'd clapped over most of her face to hide her shock. It was happy shock…he hoped, unless he'd read all the signs wrong. With only mildly shaking fingers, he removed the box from the pup's collar, throwing a treat on the floor to distract her for a moment. To his absolute delight, Minerva was still visibly reeling.

'You were trying to teach her to sit all week…for this?' she whispered.

'Sadly, it was a fruitless effort. Our dog has no sense of discipline.'

'How long have you been planning this?'

'If it had been up to me, I'd have had you wearing my ring from the moment you finally told me that you loved me. I still sometimes don't know how I've restrained myself. But I vowed to wait…to watch you become the queen you were born to be…before I asked you this one very important question.'

'Yes—the answer is yes.' She moved to reach for the ring then stopped, realising she'd interrupted him mid-speech. 'Oh, sorry… Continue.'

Liro laughed, expecting nothing less. Without breaking eye contact he sank down to one knee beside the bed, looking up at where she gloried above him in the lamplight. She had never looked more beautiful than she did at this moment, her cheeks still warmed by the afterglow of his ministrations. He had agonised over this proposal for weeks, wanting to make right all the wrongs of the first time. Wanting to give her the perfect moment she deserved…a moment worthy of a queen.

But, in the end, he'd realised that this was all that they needed—a moment that reflected who they were and who they might become as husband and wife. So long as she said yes, of course…

He took a deep breath, feeling the sheer weight of getting this moment right hit him square in his chest. 'Min, the past six months have made me happier than I had ever dreamed possible. You gave me a second chance; you gave us a second chance when most people would've simply given up. We haven't had the easiest path…but I wouldn't change it for the world.'

He opened up the box, revealing the ring that he'd had hand-designed by a jeweller in the old town. The design was a stunning gold band with a pear-shaped diamond, held in place by a swan-like symbol on one side and a graceful archer's bow on the other. The glitter in Minerva's eyes became full-on tears from the moment she saw the ring, so much so that he barely heard her gasping, 'Yes,' between wracking sobs.

'Yes?' he asked, holding her as she sank down onto her knees on their bedroom floor beside him.

'Yes!' she practically squealed, holding her hand out for him to slowly slide on the ring. Once he realised that it was a perfect fit, the bands of anxiety in his chest relaxed somewhat enough for him to claim her lips in a frantic kiss. She had worried that he would feel restricted by the return to royal life, when in reality he had never felt more at home anywhere in his life than he did in this palace.

As he looked down at his fiancée…his queen… he thanked destiny for sending them on this wayward path. He wouldn't have had it any other way.

\* \* \* \* \*

## #4129 INNOCENT'S WEDDING DAY WITH THE ITALIAN
### by Michelle Smart

Discovering that her billionaire fiancé, Enzo, will receive her inheritance if they wed, Rebecca leaves him at the altar and gives him twenty-four hours to explain himself. He vows his feelings are real, but dare Rebecca believe him and succumb to a passionate wedding night?

## #4130 THE HOUSEKEEPER'S ONE-NIGHT BABY
### by Sharon Kendrick

Letting someone close goes against Niccolò Macario's every instinct. When he receives news that shy housekeeper Lizzie Bailey, the woman he spent one scorching night with, is pregnant, Niccolò is floored—because his only thought is to find her and claim his child!

## #4131 BACK TO CLAIM HIS CROWN
*Innocent Royal Runaways*
### by Natalie Anderson

When Crown Prince Lucian returns from the dead to reclaim his throne, he stops his usurper's wedding, creating a media frenzy! He's honor-bound to provide jilted Princess Zara with shelter, and the chemistry between the ruthless royal and the virgin princess sparks an urgent, irresistible desire...

## #4132 THE DESERT KING'S KIDNAPPED VIRGIN
*Innocent Stolen Brides*
### by Caitlin Crews

When Hope Cartwright is kidnapped from her convenient wedding, she's sure she should feel outraged. But whisked away by Cyrus Ashkan, the sheikh she's been promised to from birth, Hope feels something *far* more dangerous—desire.

HPCNMRA0723

### #4133 A SON HIDDEN FROM THE SICILIAN
#### by Lorraine Hall
Wary of billionaire Lorenzo Parisi's notorious reputation, Brianna Andersen vowed to protect her baby by keeping him a secret. Now the Sicilian knows the truth, and he's determined to be a father! As their blazing chemistry reignites, Brianna must admit the real risk may be to her heart...

### #4134 HER FORBIDDEN AWAKENING IN GREECE
*The Secret Twin Sisters*
#### by Kim Lawrence
Nanny Rose Hill is surprised when irresistible CEO Zac Adamos personally proposes a job for her in Greece looking after his godson! She can't let herself get too close, but can the innocent really walk away without exploring the unforeseen passion Zac has awakened inside her?

### #4135 THEIR DIAMOND RING RUSE
#### by Bella Mason
Self-made billionaire Julian Ford needs to secure funding from a group of traditional investors. His solution: an engagement to an heiress, and Lily Barnes-Shah fits the bill perfectly! Until their mutual chemistry makes Julian crave something outside the bounds of their temporary agreement...

### #4136 HER CONVENIENT VOW TO THE BILLIONAIRE
#### by Jane Holland
When Sabrina Templeton returns to the orphanage from her childhood to stop her former sweetheart from tearing it down, playboy CEO Rafael Romano offers a shocking compromise... He'll hand it over if Sabrina becomes his convenient bride!

---

# Get 3 FREE REWARDS!

**We'll send you 2 FREE Books _plus_ a FREE Mystery Gift.**

**FREE** Value Over **$20**

Both the **Harlequin® Desire** and **Harlequin Presents®** series feature compelling novels filled with passion, sensuality and intriguing scandals.

---

**YES!** Please send me 2 FREE novels from the Harlequin Desire or Harlequin Presents series and my FREE gift (gift is worth about $10 retail). After receiving them, if I don't wish to receive any more books, I can return the shipping statement marked "cancel." If I don't cancel, I will receive 6 brand-new Harlequin Presents Larger-Print books every month and be billed just $6.30 each in the U.S. or $6.49 each in Canada, a savings of at least 10% off the cover price, or 3 Harlequin Desire books (2-in-1 story editions) every month and be billed just $7.83 each in the U.S. or $8.43 each in Canada, a savings of at least 12% off the cover price. It's quite a bargain! Shipping and handling is just 50¢ per book in the U.S. and $1.25 per book in Canada.* I understand that accepting the 2 free books and gift places me under no obligation to buy anything. I can always return a shipment and cancel at any time by calling the number below. The free books and gift are mine to keep no matter what I decide.

Choose one: ☐ **Harlequin Desire**
(225/326 BPA GRNA)

☐ **Harlequin Presents Larger-Print**
(176/376 BPA GRNA)

☐ **Or Try Both!**
(225/326 & 176/376 BPA GRQP)

Name (please print)

Address                                                                                          Apt. #

City                                        State/Province                          Zip/Postal Code

Email: Please check this box ☐ if you would like to receive newsletters and promotional emails from Harlequin Enterprises ULC and its affiliates. You can unsubscribe anytime.

Mail to the **Harlequin Reader Service:**
**IN U.S.A.:** P.O. Box 1341, Buffalo, NY 14240-8531
**IN CANADA:** P.O. Box 603, Fort Erie, Ontario L2A 5X3

**Want to try 2 free books from another series! Call 1-800-873-8635 or visit www.ReaderService.com.**

---

*Terms and prices subject to change without notice. Prices do not include sales taxes, which will be charged (if applicable) based on your state or country of residence. Canadian residents will be charged applicable taxes. Offer not valid in Quebec. This offer is limited to one order per household. Books received may not be as shown. Not valid for current subscribers to the Harlequin Presents or Harlequin Desire series. All orders subject to approval. Credit or debit balances in a customer's account(s) may be offset by any other outstanding balance owed by or to the customer. Please allow 4 to 6 weeks for delivery. Offer available while quantities last.

**Your Privacy**—Your information is being collected by Harlequin Enterprises ULC, operating as Harlequin Reader Service. For a complete summary of the information we collect, how we use this information and to whom it is disclosed, please visit our privacy notice located at corporate.harlequin.com/privacy-notice. From time to time we may also exchange your personal information with reputable third parties. If you wish to opt out of this sharing of your personal information, please visit readerservice.com/consumerschoice or call 1-800-873-8635. **Notice to California Residents**—Under California law, you have specific rights to control and access your data. For more information on these rights and how to exercise them, visit corporate.harlequin.com/california-privacy.

HDHP23

# HARLEQUIN
## PLUS

Try the best multimedia subscription service for romance readers like you!

---

## Read, Watch and Play.

Experience the easiest way to get the romance content you crave.

Start your **FREE TRIAL** at
<u>www.harlequinplus.com/freetrial</u>.